SATORi
SUNSET

A Pulp Fiction of Enlightened Adventure

Douglas John Noble

Published by Ethos Unlimited Publishing

Printed in the United States of America

First Printing, 2015

ISBN 978-0-9968700-0-9

Ethos Unlimited Publishing
www.EthosUnlimited.com

SATORi SUNSET

Story

1

2 P.M. Friday

"I need a favor," said Jeb. "It's a big one."

"Oh shit, what is it?" said Oliver.

"I need you to make a run for me," said Jeb.

"What kind of run, like a drug run or something?" laughed Oliver.

"Yeah. Just some weed," said Jeb.

"What the fuck Jeb?"

"Come on Oliver I never ask you for anything, besides this is a big deal," said Jeb.

"It's always a big deal. I've been bailing you out of shit since we were little kids. You're supposed to be my big brother, Jeb."

"Oliver, this is for real. I need you to do this for me. I will make it worth your while, $2,000 cash, plus expenses. I'm in some shit here and I need you to come through on this one."

"Fuck, fuck, fuck... What the fuck would I tell mom? What am I supposed to drive? Where the fuck do you want me to go?"

"California," said Jeb.

"No. No... There is no way in hell I'm driving to California. I have to be back to school in two weeks. Remember that thing I do every year. That thing I moved away from La Crosse for."

"Don't worry about mom, I'll help cover that. Take the van," said Jeb.

"The fucking van... You're going to take care of mom for me? Why can't you do this shit yourself?"

"I would if I could. I've got a warrant out for my arrest. I need to turn myself in in four days. I got busted with some weed a few months ago. Like two ounces. I'm going to have to sit for about a month this time. Big Roy can't know. He would flip a lid. I owe him big time. I need to make this happen."

"Big Roy, I thought you were done with that shit."

"Two grand and a free trip to California. You have two weeks before you have to go back to school. It's an adventure man. You can do this. It's not a big deal. Take some cash out, pick up some shit and head back. Simple as that. You don't even have to look in the bag. Just pretend it's not even there. "

"Ahhh.... Ahhhhhhhh.... Fine. Fuck, fine, fuuucckkkk...."

"Quiet down man. Be cool. Hey, don't tell anyone about this. You got that, nobody. Especially that fucking Charlie kid," said Jeb.

2

5 P.M. Friday

"So my brother wants me to go on a trip for him," said Oliver.

"What kind of a trip? What do you mean," said Charlie.

"He wants me to go on a drug run."

"What? A fucking drug run?" said Charlie excitedly. "Like a mule, like heroine and crack and shit?"

"No, I'm not a mule. And it's just weed."

"Just weed. Just weed. You're going to be a fucking drug mule."

"Shut up dude. I knew I shouldn't have told you," said Oliver.

"Well when are we supposed to leave?" asked Charlie.

"No way dude. I'm leaving. Not we."

"You mean to tell me, you're going on the road trip of your life by yourself and leaving me here? No way man, I'm not going to miss this," said Charlie.

"There is no way I can take you Charlie. I wasn't even supposed to tell you. I'm not even supposed to be doing this. My brother is apparently in debt to this guy Big Roy, and he's supposed to be doing this thing. The problem is he can't do it himself, because he's in a bunch of trouble here."

"You have to take me," said Charlie. "You can barely make it to Madison without having a shit fit about the traffic and the distance and you make that trip every two weeks."

"This shit is for real Charlie. It's not a joke this time. There is going to be a crap ton of money and real weed. A lot of it."

"Come on man, you need me. You've never been out of the state by yourself. It's a long drive. How many hours do you think it is? It's a lot right? It will take a couple of days just to drive there. I can be your wing man. Your tire man. Help you drive and keep you from falling asleep at the wheel."

"Shit. This day just keeps getting worse. I'm not even supposed to be telling you about this. You can't tell anyone about this, Charlie. You got that."

"Come on Oliver, I'm your best friend, we've known each other since kindergarten. You know the only way I'll be able to keep my mouth shut is if I'm with you."

"Dude, fuck...Shit fuck!"

"This is gonna be so cool man. We're like fucking outlaws," said Charlie.

"If you come you can't tell anyone about this, ever. No one can know. I'm not supposed to be doing this."

"How long is it going to take, aren't you supposed to be back in school in like two weeks?"

"I don't know. It shouldn't take too long. I google mapped it. Google said it's like 34 hours each way. So figuring in for sleep I should be able to do it in like 5 day's tops," said Oliver.

"You mean us hombre. We are like the two amigos in this thing. We are going to ride off in the sunset, and we are going to get laid," said Charlie.

"What? No... We are not going to get laid. We are going to drive. We are going to be there for like twenty minutes, an hour tops. I don't know, however long it takes us to give them whatever and get whatever and get the fuck home in one piece."

"The two Amigos. Is that a thing or something? We need code names," said Charlie.

3

7 P.M. Friday Night

"I'm going to take one final trip before the summer mom," Oliver said.

"One final trip? You never take trips, Oliver," said his mom. "I think you should just stay home and spend a little time with your mother. I know as soon as you graduate you're going to go off and get some high powered job, who knows where and leave me here to fend for myself. Don't even tell me that your brother would look after me. I love him with all my heart, but you and I both know he's not good like you are. You're my little baby and you always will be. You know that."

"Mom, I'm taking the van."

"The van... Oh, I see, you want to take the van. Just how far do you plan on going on this little trip of yours?"

"I'm going to California mom. I'm taking a trip to California. I want to see the ocean before I go back to school."

"Oh Oliver... My little Oliver... Have you ever seen the ocean? No. No, you haven't seen the ocean. And do you know why? Because we could never afford to fly there. Do you have any idea how far away the ocean is? I will tell you. It's a hell of a long ways away. You can't just drive to the ocean. You have to plan. You have to, well, you have to plan for a long, long time. You can't just one day say, 'I want to go to the ocean,' just because you have some sort of fancy to shake your tail feathers in the breeze."

"So you don't want me to take the van?"

"My boy, Oliver," his mom said softly, gently swaying her head from side to side.

"I'm only going to be gone for a few days mom. I google mapped it and it's about 36 hours one way."

"Oh, I see, Google. You Googled it. Google might know a lot, but your little old mom knows a thing or two too. Did Google tell you that you could be raped or killed along the way? Did, Google tell you that? I know you don't want to hear this, and it breaks my heart to think about it, or god forbid tell you. There are men out there, grown men, who will actually rape other men," she whispered. "I saw it on Lifetime. There are these men they call serial rapists, who just go around raping everything they see, men or women it doesn't even matter. I do not want to see my little baby boy on lifetime telling his horrific story of how he was raped by a gang of serial rapers. I will not stand for it."

"Mom, if I can't take the van I will have to borrow Charlie's Geo Metro. Please can I take the van? I promise I won't get raped. I need to do this mom."

"Oh Oliver, you poor innocent child. There is so much you need to learn about this world. You just turned 21 and you think you have it all figured out. I tell you, I'm 44 and I still haven't figured all of it out yet. I'm almost there. But some days I still don't know," his mother drifted off. "Wait, Charlie's little shit box. You can't take that little blue turd. You'll break down somewhere along the highway in the middle of the night and get eaten by a bear."

"So I can take the van."

"Oliver, you don't know how much time you have left with me. Fine… Fine… You think you're so grown up. You think you can handle yourself in this big wide world I've been protecting you from all these years. Fine, take the van," Oliver's mom said, now openly sobbing into her hands. "Just be careful."

"Thanks mom. I love you."

"Make sure you bring your cell phone," she said rubbing the tears from her eyes with both hands. "I'm going to call you every day. If I call you twice a day I want to you to answer. Don't just pretend I'm not calling."

"Okay mom. I got it. I'm leaving in the morning okay."

"I'll make you pancakes."

4

6 A.M. Saturday

Knocking on Oliver's door.

"Wake up, open the door," whispered Jeb. "I don't want to wake up mom." Jeb quietly knocked again. "Come on man. Open up the door."

"What, what's up?" Oliver slowly woke to the realization that Jeb was whispering and quietly knocking on his door.

"Come in."

"I can't it's locked," Jeb said as Oliver slipped out of bed and let him in.

"What's up," asked Oliver, scratching his head. "I've never seen you awake this early in the morning. What time is it anyway?"

"Why do you lock your door?"

"So mom can't just walk in. What time is it?"

"Yeah, probably a good idea, I can't even count how many times she walked in on me jerking off. I think that's why she doesn't trust me."

"So what are you doing here?" Oliver asked.

"I've got everything you need here for your trip."

"What do you mean? What do I need?"

"You think they're just going to let you walk in and take 60 lbs of weed?"

"Shhhh.... Wait, what?"

"Here. Take this bag. It has the money for the stuff, a list of what you need and some cash for the trip."

"I need a list," Oliver asks rubbing his eyes.

"A list of the different strains you need and the amounts of each," said Jeb.

"What do you mean different strains?" Oliver looked at the list. 15 lbs Sour Diesel, 10 lbs Hawaiian Sunshine, 15 lbs Jamaican Thunder, 10 lbs Jimmy Dean, 10 lbs Mambo #3.

"Don't worry about it, just take it," said Jeb in a frustrated tone. "Take the whole bag. The money is in there and a list, and this is for your expenses on the trip," Jeb said handing Oliver a small folded bundle of cash. "It's twelve hundred dollars. It should...it better, cover your gas and food for the whole thing."

"How much money is this?" asked Oliver.

"It's $150,000. Don't worry about that though. Don't look at it. Don't touch it. Don't even think about it. Put it in the back and forget it's there until you have to pull it out and give it to Jack."

"Holy shit Jeb. $150,000? Do you have any idea how long mom would have to work to make $150,000? I saw her taxes last year, she makes like $16,000 in a whole year."

"Don't worry about it. Just drive out and hand this whole bag to Jack. Jack will take care of the rest."

"Jack, you make it sound so easy. Just give the bag to Jack. Who the fuck is Jack?"

"Here's the address," Jeb said, handing Oliver a piece of paper. "One more thing," said Jeb. "Don't call me."

"What do you mean, don't call you?" asked Oliver.

"I don't trust the phones. The cops can trace that shit. I've been dealing with some high profile guys."

"I don't know if I can do this Jeb."

"Oliver, you have this under control. I would do it if I could, but I need your help here. When you get the shit just hide it under the compartment in the floor of the van. You know, where the back seats are supposed to fold into. Just put it in there and forget about it. Put a mental barrier over that floor and don't think about it. If you start to think about it, it will drive you crazy. It's like walking a tight rope, or climbing a mountain. Don't look down."

"I told mom."

"What? You fucking told mom!"

"No, no I told her I'm going to California because I want to see the ocean before I go back to school," said Oliver.

"Oh, well you better not tell mom. Ever. I mean never. She would crucify me. Speaking of mom... You better get out of here before she wants to make you pancakes or some shit. That would take all day. When you get there," said Jeb, "Just tell them you're here for Big Roy."

5

7 A.M. Saturday

Oliver walked up the three flights of stairs to Charlie's apartment, and knocked on the door.

"I thought you'd never get here," said Charlie opening the door with a grin from ear to ear. "Help me carry my shit."

"What shit?"

"All my shit for the trip," said Charlie. "I'm not going to California with just a tooth brush and pair of flip-flops."

"Fine, but we need to make it quick," Oliver said looking down at the pile of things on the floor. "What is all this? I don't take this much stuff when I leave for the year to college. Whatever," said Oliver, "let's just load this shit up and go."

6

8 A.M. Saturday

"So where are we going?" said Charlie.

"We're going to California," said Oliver.

"I mean where in California are we going."

"I've got the address right here," said Oliver. I guess it's this place called Trinidad. It's in Humboldt County."

"Holy shit, Humboldt County? Did you see that movie about Humboldt County? Everybody there is fucking crazy, they all smoke weed and grow it and live off the land and shit."

"No, I didn't see it. Movies are movies. You can't base a real opinion of a place on a movie."

7

10 A.M. Saturday

For the first couple of hours the miles tick by and everything seems like it was in slow motion, everything was new. They noticed signs alongside the road and every car was different.

"So what does your mom think of this," asked Charlie?

"She thinks I'm gonna get raped by a bear," said Oliver.

"She thinks you're going to get raped by a large hairy gay man?" said Charlie.

"Yep, pretty much," said Oliver.

12 P.M. Saturday in Iowa

"Have you ever met this Big Roy guy," asked Charlie?

"I've never met him but my brother has been talking about him for years. Well, he mentions him every once in a while anyway. He likes to tell me stories about the shit Big Roy has been up to. Most of it seems like bullshit to me though. I don't think I would want to mess with the guy."

"I heard Big Roy killed a guy for touching his girlfriend's ass," said Charlie.

"Whatever, who did you hear that from?"

"I heard it from a guy at the sandwich shop I work at. It was his cousin. I guess Big Roy got away with it, if he's having us do this job."

"He's not having us do this job. My brother is having us do this job. My fucking brother," said Oliver.

"Your brother is the coolest dude I know," said Charlie.

"My brother has been leaving me to pick up his shit since I was a kid. It used to be little shit. Like when he was 15 and I was 10, he broke the Play Station jumping around the living room on a pogo stick. He talked me into taking the fall for it since I was mom's favorite and he thought I would get in less trouble."

"Did you get in trouble," asked Charlie?

"No he was pretty much right. In mom's eyes back then I could do no wrong. But that's not the point," said Oliver. Then like two years later, as soon as he graduated he just left me alone with her. He ran off to Oregon to work on a ski hill or whatever. When he left it all changed. All the shit mom used to pile on Jeb ended up on me."

"I remember that," said Charlie. "Your brother is always going on crazy adventures."

"Adventures? You mean running away."

"Hey man, your brother is pretty cool. I think you're feeling sorry for yourself. Hasn't he helped you out quite a bit with money for college? Besides, in case you haven't noticed all these years we've been best friends I didn't wake up with a golden ticket either."

"At least you had two parents who were always there," said Oliver.

"That's what you saw. Shit, when my parents weren't fighting they were at the bar spending all our money. At least your mom isn't a drunk. Remember when we were kids and I got that TV in my bedroom. I think my dad got it from a friend or something, I don't even remember anymore."

"Yeah, I remember that we used to stay up all night watching reruns. Didn't it get stolen or something."

"My mom sold it. Her brother, my uncle, came right into my room, turned it off and took it. Fuckers. I had to sit home and play Connect 4 by myself all night, while my parents went to the bar."

3 P.M. Saturday Nebraska

"So this is Nebraska."

6 P.M. Saturday Nebraska

"Nebraska sucks," said Charlie.

"How do people live here?" said Oliver. "It would be hard to live in this wide open land. What would you do all the time? Everything looks the same."

"Hey, I need to pee," said Charlie.

"Just wait a few minutes till we see an exit."

"I don't know if I can," said Charlie. "I gotta go man. Just pull over here."

"We can't pull over here."

"Why can't we pull over here?"

"It's illegal to just pull over on the interstate," said Oliver.

"I gotta fucking pee dude. Really bad."

"Pee in a cup or something."

"We threw away all the cups when we stopped to eat, no bottles, no cups nothing. Who cares if it's illegal, I'm going to pee my fucking pants."

"Charlie, we have $150,000 in a duffel bag back there. I can't risk getting pulled over."

"What? Did I hear that right? How much did you say we have in a duffel bag in the back?"

"$150,000"

"I gotta pee, I gotta pee, I gotta pee. Don't make me pee my pants, you're my best friend."

"Didn't you bring a Thermos," asked Oliver."

"I'm not going to pee in my Thermos," said Charlie, almost crying now.

"Pee in the Thermos man. You can do it."

"What if there isn't enough room?"

"Pinch it off," said Oliver, "then dump it out the window, and finish."

"Fine, fine mother fucker. But you're buying me a new Thermos."

Charlie climbed between the front seats grabbed the Thermos and headed to the back of the van. "Oh shit, it's almost full. I'm not done yet," he yelled.

"Pinch it off," said Oliver.

"EEEmMMmm... Ouch... Now what do I do," said Charlie, squirming around holding the Thermos in one hand and his crotch with the other.

"Dump it out the window."

"Roll the window down!" yelled Charlie.

"It doesn't roll down. It only opens a crack." Oliver hit the button and the back window butterflied open two inches at the back.

"How am I supposed to dump pee out that?"

"Shit man, you gotta come up here and dump it."

Charlie tipped the thermos and tried to dump it out the crack in the back of the window. The wind caught it and blew most of it back into the van. A large stream ran down the inside of the window. Charlie was getting showered with pee, but now he was committed. Dripping with pee, Charlie once again aimed and filled the Thermos to the top.

"Oh no," Charlie whimpered to himself. Once again pinching it off and tipping the Thermos out the crack of the window. Again, he was sprayed in the face and chest and a large amount just spilled down the inside of the window. He stilled himself for one last push.

"What are you doing back there?" asked Oliver.

"Peeing," said Charlie.

"I know you're peeing. What in the world is happening?"

Charlie sat back in the seat and replaced the lid on the half full steaming Thermos of pee.

"Pee, Oliver! I got it in my face. I got pee in my mouth man. It went in my mouth," said Charlie on the verge of tears.

"How did you get pee in your mouth?" asked Oliver.

"The wind. The wind blew it back in on me," said Charlie, climbing back up into the front seat.

"You're soaking wet," said Oliver. "Why didn't you just come up here and dump it out the front window? I could have rolled it down all the way. You could have stuck your arm out."

"You know I don't like anyone to see me naked."

"I wouldn't have looked man. Check it out Charlie, there's an exit. We can pull over at this truck stop and you can clean up."

"I got piss all over myself," Charlie whimpered. "It's in my hair."

8 P.M. Saturday Nebraska

"Look Charlie," Oliver said, "I won't tell anyone."

"I told you I don't want to talk about it," said Charlie.

"You haven't said a word for two hours now," said Oliver.

"Did you say we have $100,000 in here with us?"

"No."

"Bullshit. How much was is it?"

"$150,000"

"No fucking way," said Charlie.

"Yep."

"I want to see it," said Charlie.

"No, you can't see it."

"Where is it?"

"You can't see it Charlie. We can't touch it."

"Have you seen it?" asked Charlie.

"No, I haven't seen it. Only the bag. I was told not to look at it, or think about it, or touch it. That's what I intend to do. $150,000 is way more trouble than I want deal with."

"Don't be a pussy," said Charlie. "I'm gonna look. Where is it?"

"No way," said Oliver, as Charlie leaped between the seats and into the back of the van. "Stay up here. Get buckled back in," said Oliver. "It's totally illegal to be unbuckled when we're driving."

"Where is it Oliver," said Charlie rooting around in the back, jumping from seat to seat to get a better vantage point. "I'm going to find it. You might as well just tell me where it is."

Charlie noticed the flaps where the van's middle seats folded into the floor. He knelt next to the hole and lifted up the cover. Underneath was a large black backpack.

"Holy shit," Charlie whispered, in awe. "This is the fucking lottery right here. You win this on 'Am I Smarter than a Fifth Grader' and you're the happiest guy in the world. "This is for real man," said Charlie, talking in a quiet cautious tone. Slowly, meticulously, Charlie reached down and gently grasped the bag. He lifted it out feeling the weight.

"Put it back Charlie," yelled Oliver, temporarily breaking Charlie's spell. Charlie didn't answer. "Put it back Charlie. We can't mess with that shit. If something happens to that bag do you have any idea how much shit we would be in? Big Roy would chop off our fucking dicks. Starting with mine."

"Who's going to know?" said Charlie, climbing back into the front seat, grinning.

"I'm going to pull over. Put it back."

"Bullshit. You can't pull over. It's illegal. Remember," said Charlie, reaching down and unzipping the bag. "Whoa..." Charlie reached into the pack and grabbed a large rubber banded bundle. "How much do you think this is? This stack right here in my hand?"

"I don't know," said Oliver? "A couple of thousand dollars I guess."

"Slap me in the face with it," said Charlie.

"What?"

"Slap me in the face with this bundle of money." Charlie poked at Oliver with a large bundle of cash.

"You're nuts dude. For real?"

"I'm dead serous man," said Charlie. "Just do it."

"Fine." Oliver grabbed the bundle of cash and slapped Charlie as hard as he could right across the face. Instantly Charlie started gushing blood from his nose.

"What the fuck dude," yelled Charlie. "You hit me right in my nose."

"You told me to slap you in the face with it."

"Not in the nose. The nose isn't the face."

"Fuck the semantics. You're bleeding all over the money dude."

"What do I do?" said Charlie.

"Get the money off your lap. Plug your nose."

"Plug it with what."

"Your fingers, I don't know."

Charlie threw the bag behind them and tipped his head back to plug it with his fingers as well as he could. There was blood all over the front of his shirt, and on his hands.

"The glove box. I think there are napkins in the glove box," said Oliver.

Charlie reached down with slippery bloody hands and clawed open the glove box to find two napkins.

"This isn't going to cut it man," said Charlie.

"Dude. Go back in the back and use a shirt or something," said Oliver.

Charlie scrambled to the back and dug out a towel from his bag.

"You hit me with the bills in the palm of your hand, right on the middle of my face Oliver. You were supposed to slap me on the cheek or something with the ends of the money," said Charlie.

"How am I supposed to know how to hit someone in the face with a stack of money? Besides, I'm trying to drive. Why in the world would you want me to hit you with the money?"

"Just kind of a fantasy I guess," said Charlie. "Sounded like a good idea at the time."

"You need to get that money cleaned up Charlie. That blood all over it is probably not a good thing."

7.5

10 P.M. Saturday

"We need to find a place to sleep," said Oliver. "I'm getting tired. I need a break."

"Let me drive," said Charlie. "We can trade off. You sleep while I drive."

"I don't know man," said Oliver. "You haven't slept all day either. I think we should get a hotel."

"I'm not tired Oliver. Let me drive."

"Alright, but if you get tired wake me up."

They hopped off I80 in Cheyenne, Wyoming. The wind was howling across the planes when they stepped out to fill the tank and stretch their now stiff bodies. Gusts of wind seemed to want to tip the van. Several loose pieces of paper and a green soda bottle skipped across the shadowy parking lot. They were the only vehicle at this small gas station just off the interstate. The pumps were all old and, like almost all of the gas stations along I80, they were prepay. Oliver and Charlie both went in.

The old man behind the counter was wearing an old Stetson cowboy hat and faded, tan Carhartt work jacket.

"You boys aren't from around here," the old man said from across the store to both of them, but neither one in particular.

Charlie was milling around between the candy isle and the potato chip isle, and Oliver was trying to find something to drink. He picked out a bottle of Coke and it seemed to have a light coating of dust on it. He thought that was weird since it was inside a cooler.

"Where you boys headed," asked the old man?

"California," said Charlie. "We hear there's gold out there."

"Ha. Ha." The man chuckled. "Gold... Nothin' but hippies and gays. I was stationed there in the army back in 1960. All the gold in the world couldn't get me to go back to that god forsaken nightmare. Those people are all crazy."

"My friend Oliver here," said Charlie, "wants to see the ocean before he goes back to college in a couple of weeks."

"Now why in the world would you want to do something foolish like that," said the old man. "I tell you what. Kids these days are nothin' but trouble. Smokin' all that marijuana. Can you believe they made that crap legal in Colorado? I tell you what. It ain't legal here in Wyoming. They catch you with that shit here and they'll string you up by your balls and leave you there for the crows."

"We'll take $60 on pump 3," said Oliver.

"So you're the ring leader for this little excursion?" asked the man.

"Yes sir," said Oliver.

"Yes sir," echoed the man. "You listen to me kid," said the old man, quiet now. "You two ain't pretty enough to be fags, and you look too stupid to be hippies. I can tell when somethings up though, I've always had a sense for it. You boys watch yourselves. Not everybody around here is as nice as me. There's a lot of young guys like you coming through here bringing the pot up out of Colorado an infectin' our young. It ain't just the cops out here you boys got to worry about. There's a lot of places a couple of upstanding boys such as yourself could get lost out on the planes, if you catch my drift."

"We're just here to get some gas, sir," said Oliver.

"He... Heeee..." cackled the old man. "You boys here about that Interstate 80 killer? He's been traveling up and down this here highway pickin' off people stopped along the side of the road. Got some folks just west of here a few days ago. Don't get killed boys."

Oliver and Charlie crossed the dark parking lot back to the car and practically jumped in, like a kid trying to jump back into bed without getting his feet grabbed by someone who might be underneath. A large gust of wind rocked the van as Oliver started the engine.

"Holy shit that was spooky," said Charlie.

"He was full of shit. He was just trying to scare us," said Oliver.

Oliver remembered back to when he was a kid spending the night at his Cousin Leah's house. They heard a noise outside and she was scared. He told her that he had made the noise to make her feel better so she could go back to sleep. He lay in bed awake for the rest of the night, and she fell right back to sleep.

"Yeah," said Charlie. "He's probably full of shit."

"I'm going to keep driving for a while," said Oliver.

As they drove down the highway the headlights shot a beam just far enough into the distance to see the road ahead. The white painted center line dotted along and the green mile marker signs ticked by.

"What if we get caught," said Charlie after a long silence.

"We're not going to get caught," said Oliver.

"Maybe your mom was right about getting raped by bears," said Charlie.

"Can we not talk about this," said Oliver.

"Are you thinking about it" asked Charlie.

"No," said Oliver. "I don't want to think about it."

"Holy shit," said Charlie. "Check it out. It's the continental divide. Let's stop and piss on it."

They entered the little pull off at the side of the freeway. The wind blew a steady cool breeze through the darkness.

"Check it out," said Charlie. "The divide must be up there by that sign. I heard that if you piss on this side everything goes in the Atlantic Ocean and if you piss on that side everything goes in the Pacific. Let's walk over there."

"I don't know man. We should just piss here and get back on the road."

"Where's your heuvos man," Charlie said running to the sign. Oliver followed.

"I'm pissing on the Atlantic," said Oliver. "Fuck that side."

"I'm pissing on the Pacific for good luck," said Charlie, whipping it out and spreading a steady stream back and forth in the sand.

"AAAAHHHHhhhhh!!!!!!   AAAAAAAAAAAhhhhhhhhhhhhHH!!! AAaaaaaaaaaHHHHHHhhh!!!!" Oliver yelled a long primal scream into the night.

"Holy shit man," said Charlie. "Let it out. What the fuck was that scream all about?"

"I don't know," said Oliver, sinking down into a squat and wrapping his arms around his knees.

"Are you crying?" asked Charlie. Oliver didn't answer. They just sat there. Oliver squatting into his arms, and Charlie looking off into the dark open nothing. After about 15 minutes, a minivan pulled into the turn off.

"Hey Oliver, get down. We gotta hide."

"Why?"

"The I80 Killer."

Both boys ducked into a ditch just ahead.

"Do you think he saw us?" asked Charlie.

"How should I know," whispered Oliver.

"He's not getting out. I knew that old dude was on to something. Maybe he works with this guy, maybe he fucking called him."

"Chill out Charlie. We'll just sit here till he leaves."

"That old dude was some kind of bad omen. I don't want to die."

"Nobody is going to die."

"It's cold out here Oliver."

A howl of wind passed a pile of rocks in the distance. Oliver and Charlie shivered in their t-shirts. Five minutes passed, and then ten, the minivan just sat there in the darkness.

"Oliver, what are we going to do?"

"Maybe it's just someone pulling off to sleep for the night. This place is called a rest area. Let's just sneak up to our van, hop in and get outta here."

They crept along the ditch to the front of the van, as a couple of cars passed by on the dark highway.

"Okay Charlie, as soon as the next car comes by we'll bolt up to the van, you on your side me on the driver's side. We'll get in and go."

"Works for me," said Charlie, heart pounding like it could beat through his chest at any moment.

"Here it comes," whispered Oliver. "Three, two, one go!"

The boys scrambled up the loose rocks of the ditch as the headlights of the car whooshed by on the pavement.

"Fuck, Oliver it's locked."

"Hold on, I've got the key."

"You didn't have it ready?"

"I thought I did. Fuck, I dropped it. It was in my hand. Oh shit. It must be close."

"Oh shit," said Charlie panting now. "We're gonna die."

Just then the driver's side door of the other minivan opened.

Charlie and Oliver started to scream. "AAAHHh…"

"You guys all right?" said the man stepping out of the minivan.

As the door of his van opened the lights inside illuminated his family—a small boy and young girl were sleeping in the back and a woman slept soundly in the front seat.

"We're ah, just trying to get into our van," said Charlie.

"I think I dropped the key, said Oliver."

"Let me give you a hand, I have a flash light," said the man.

"Thanks," said Oliver.

"Where do you think you dropped it," asked the man?

"Over here in this gravel, I think," said Oliver.

The man shone his light in front of the van down into the gravel of the ditch. "There they are," he said. "What were you guys doing down there?"

"We were just checking out the Continental Divide," said Charlie.

They thanked the man, hopped back into the van and pulled onto the highway.

"Why did you lock it?" asked Charlie.

"Habit I guess," said Oliver.

"What happened out there with the screaming thing, Oliver? Are you okay?"

"I don't want to talk about it," said Oliver.

They drove in silence for a long stretch.

"Are you getting tired yet." asked Charlie.

"Yeah, a little," said Oliver glancing down at the clock. 1:00 A.M.

"I can drive for a while," said Charlie. "I'm pretty good at pulling all-nighters. Remember when I worked at the bread factory downtown? Sometimes I stayed up for two or three days at a time."

"All right," said Oliver. "For a few hours."

They pulled off on an empty exit. There were no lights around as far as the eye could see. The stars were bright in the sky above.

"Look at all those stars, Oliver."

They both looked up, transfixed.

"I've never seen that many stars," said Charlie. "Is that the Milky Way?"

"We're just a tiny speck," said Oliver. "We are almost nothing."

A set of headlights on other side of the highway broke their reverence.

"We better get going," said Oliver.

They got back into the car and Oliver fell asleep, as Charlie drove on. West.

8

6 A.M. Sunday

Oliver woke with the sun rising at his back. As he stretched he saw a sign that read, "Drowsy Driving Causes Crashes," and thought it was odd. Ahead of them as far as Oliver could see, stretched a long, straight, flat open expanse of highway bordered on both sides with white flat salt.

"This must be the salt flats," said Oliver, as if to no one in particular.

"What was that," said Charlie.

"The salt flats," said Oliver. "Way over there is the great salt lake. These salt flats are amazing. Could you imagine crossing them on horseback, or even on foot? Somewhere on these salt flats they have the Bonneville races every year. They're these races where they try to break land speed records. Charlie. Hey Charlie?"

"What? How much meat would that require?"

"Pull over, I'm driving."

"But there isn't an exit."

"Just pull over, Charlie."

"I did see a sign that said, 'Drowsy Drivers Pull Over If Necessary,' but I thought I was dreaming."

Oliver hopped back into the driver's seat and headed west over the salt flats. The sky over the tiny looking mountain range in the distance shone pink and purple and traversed into a magical dreamy blue.

After an hour and a half of long straight, seemingly endless driving across the salt flats Oliver understood what the signs were for. Still they headed west, always west. An endless cycle of men headed west to conquer, find fortune. West through the savages. West for plunder and pillage. West for the gold rush. West on an epic quest for the green gold.

"I need a cheeseburger," announced Charlie.

"I haven't seen an exit for a while," said Oliver.

"What time is it," asked Charlie.

"About 11:00 A.M.," said Oliver.

"Where are we?"

"Somewhere in Nevada," said Oliver. "I think we're a couple of hours from California."

"Holy shit, I need a cheeseburger," said Charlie.

"We should be in Reno a little bit after noon, can you wait to stop till we get there," asked Oliver.

"Reno, like Reno 911? I heard you can gamble and get hookers in Reno."

"Yeah, I guess so," said Oliver.

"You know what I've been thinking," said Charlie. "Why couldn't we take just one small bundle of money? They wouldn't even miss it, and if they did they just might think they forgot it."

"No," said Oliver.

"Just hear me out. We take the money to Reno. Put the whole thing on black, or whatever, and let it ride. If we win, we double our money. If we lose, we aren't out anything. They forgot to put it in the bag."

"That's just like you Charlie. If it isn't yours it has no real value. Even if it is yours it has no value. Charlie, you're the most irresponsible person I know. That's why my brother didn't want you to come with me on this trip. You don't care about anyone but yourself and you do a shitty job taking care of that."

"Fuck you Oliver. You're uptight all the time. You can't get out of your own head long enough to see anyone else around you. Poor Oliver, how is he going to get his midterm done, poor Oliver can't get laid cause he can't talk to girls without going numb in the head."

"Oh, like you are any better at talking to women? How many girlfriends have you had? How many times have you gotten laid? Not just lying about it, for real."

"PPfff... I've gotten laid."

"Yeah, when?"

"Shut up dude," said Charlie. "Okay, I've only been laid once. Remember our senior year in high school. That girl they called Snaggle Tooth, her real name was Diane. We were at a party and both of us were really drunk. It was on a dare. She pretty much did all the work. I tried to talk to her after, but I puked all over the side of the bed. She got really grossed out. She never talked to me again."

"So you did fuck Snaggle Tooth. See I thought that was a lie. What about all the 'chicks' you've been meeting on line," asked Oliver. "I thought you've met a bunch of girls."

"Well, not exactly a bunch. Honestly, I met one," said Charlie. "She wasn't what I was expecting. She was really big. Not that big girls are bad, I mean, I don't know what I mean, but she was pretty aggressive. We met for coffee. She wanted to go right up to my place. I wasn't exactly ready for that. I guess I didn't know how the whole thing was supposed to go down. In my head I was thinking we would meet for a few dates, get to know each other, then you know...do it. But she just wanted to get to it. My apartment was a shit hole as usual. I didn't want to bring her up there. I just made up some excuse and said I had to be somewhere. We exchanged numbers, but the number she gave me didn't work. I tried messaging her back online, but she never got back to me."

"Why do you lie about that shit?" asked Oliver. "I'm your best friend man. You don't have to lie to me."

"Yeah, you're my best friend in the world. I want you to think I'm cool. Who wants their best friend to be a loser?"

"You're not a loser, Charlie. We've known each other since 1st grade. Why would I keep hanging out with you all these years if I thought you were a loser?"

"Because you're a loser too," said Charlie.

There was a long pause. Reno appeared before them out of the desert and went by in flashes. Traffic lanes expanded as in most large cities. Cars, many many cars, and many many people, doing whatever people do. In the distance were large hotels with lights that flash and throb and attract the moths of the night to the many wonders within.

"I could really use a cheeseburger," said Charlie.

"We can pull off here," said Oliver.

2:00 P.M. Sunday

The sun was high over the desert. To the west, the Sierra Nevada mountain range climbed from the ground.

"Where are we?" asked Charlie, as they headed west again along the I80.

"We're almost to California," said Oliver.

"Check it out," said Charlie. "A sign for Donner Pass. Remember that story, about how they got stuck in the snow and had to eat people to survive?"

"I remember," said Oliver. "I remember they were led west by a greedy madman."

"Alright fucker," said Charlie. "Enough of this negative talk, you're not a madman."

"You know this shit we're doing is illegal right," said Oliver.

"Yeah, man, I do."

"You know they can lock us up for this shit right," said Oliver. "Fuck my brother."

"Yeah, I know all this shit. You didn't exactly beg me to come along," said Charlie, "I came all on my own. I came because I have been sitting on my ass in that same fucking spot for way too long. At least we are doing something, Oliver. We're on an adventure. An epic adventure across the country. I wouldn't miss this for anything. You may be a loser, I may be a loser, but fuck it you're the closest thing that I have to a brother and that shit matters. If you're in this shit, I'm in this shit. Let's not waste it man. If we do go down, let's have some fun before we go."

"Ready or not, here we are," said Oliver, as they passed the sign that said, 'Welcome to California.'

3 P.M. Sunday

"So what about those code names," asked Charlie?

"What code names?"

"We need code names. This guy isn't going to know us. Are we supposed to be your brother or something," asked Charlie.

"Shit, I didn't think about that yet," said Oliver. "Honestly, I don't know who I'm supposed to be. My brother is supposed to be doing this thing. Maybe I am supposed to be him."

"But there are two of us," said Charlie. "I wanna be Tango, you can be Cash."

"That's the stupidest thing I've ever heard," said Oliver. "No, no way."

"How about you are Clark and I am Kent," said Charlie.

"That's the same person," said Oliver, "Clark Kent is Super Man."

"Come on man, you're not coming up with anything," said Charlie.

"If I were to come up with something, which I'm not, it wouldn't be something from a TV action hero duo. Besides, what's the point of making up names? This guy is a drug dealer, who is he going to tell? If we do something wrong he's more likely to kill us than turn us into the cops and tell them our names."

"That is true, but what if he decides to hunt us down. If we give him our real names he will be able to find us. Google is a powerful thing, you can find anything about anybody," said Charlie.

"What reason would he have," said Oliver, "we have money, he has weed, what else is there? My brother may be a dick hole, but he wouldn't send me into a situation where I'm gonna to get killed...I don't think?"

"Well I want to be called Clark," said Charlie. "I don't want this dude to know my name."

"Whatever Charlie," said Oliver, "I'll call you whatever you want me to call you. I'm getting tired again. You're going to have to drive for a while so I can take a nap."

They pulled off at an exit in the mountains, filled up with gas and grabbed some snacks. Charlie hoped in the driver's seat.

"Call me Jeb," said Oliver, dozing off, "he's probably expecting my brother, just call me Jeb."

5 P.M. Sunday

"Where are we?" asked Oliver, just barely coming out of his slumber.

"Sacramento," said Charlie.

"Fuck Charlie, I think we're too far south," said Oliver pulling out his phone and consulting the map. "Hit I5 North and get off at Williams. You got that."

"Yeah, I got it," said Charlie.

"Wake me up when we get to Williams," said Oliver dozing off again.

6 P.M. Sunday

"We're in Williams," said Charlie.

They headed west on California Highway 20, past farm land, around what seem to be endless corners, over hills, and met up with Highway 101 at Redwood Valley, where they headed north.

8 P.M. Sunday

"How far do you think we are from where we're going?" asked Charlie.

"Check the map, I guess," said Oliver. "We're in Willits now."

"According to this, we have about 3 hours," said Charlie. "Do you think he's going to mind us showing up at his house at 11 o'clock?"

"I don't know," said Oliver. "I don't exactly have his phone number."

"Why didn't you get his phone number," said Charlie.

"Jeb is paranoid," said Oliver. "He doesn't want me to call him. He thinks his phone is bugged or something."

"Who's phone? The guy or Jeb's?" asked Charlie.

"I don't know, from what I gathered, both," said Oliver.

"What? Are there cameras, or cops sitting outside his house? Is this a sting operation or something?" said Charlie.

"I doubt it. I don't know. How should I know," said Oliver. "I know pretty much as much as you know Charlie. We are supposed to go to this address and talk to Jack."

"You make it sound so easy," said Charlie. "I wasn't freaking out before, but now I'm freaking out a little."

"I need you to keep it together Charlie," said Oliver. "It's going to be simple. We go meet this Jack guy. We pick up the shit. Then we go find somewhere to get a good night's rest. Tomorrow we drive back. It's that easy."

"Okay," said Charlie. "Okay, we can do this. Go meet Jack. Pick up the shit. Go find someplace to sleep for the night. Easy."

9 P.M. Sunday

As the last light of the sun faded into the dark of the trees, Oliver and Charlie reached the Humboldt County line.

9

They crossed over the Eel River and passed the One Log House, with the house made of the stump of one large Redwood tree. Up through the Redwood Highway section of the 101, through Richardson Grove Park where the towering trees skirt the narrow winding road so close you can almost reach out and touch them. Up they drove, past the little towns of Garberville and Redway, Miranda, Scotia, Reo Dell, through Fortuna and Fields Landing, before entering Eureka the Humboldt County seed. Still up, though Arcata and McKinleyville and for the first time on their journey, alongside the mighty Pacific Ocean.

It was too dark to see the ocean, but the ocean didn't have to be seen to be felt. It drew at them like a moth to a flame, daring them to come inside.

"I think this is the road," said Oliver.

"Big Lagoon Park Road," said Charlie, reading the sign. "Have you ever seen that movie 'Creature from the Black Lagoon'? That scared the shit out of me when I was a kid. Or that movie 'The Blue Lagoon,' with Brooke Shields? That was the first time I ever saw tits on TV."

"Shhh..." said Oliver. "I'm trying to concentrate. We're looking for Oceanview Drive."

"Is that it up there," whispered Charlie.

They took a left onto Oceanview Drive. For the first time, they saw the ocean.

"Oliver look," Charlie said, still whispering. "It's the Ocean."

There it was…deep and wide and black. From over 238,000 miles away the moon stood in the sky, casting a soft glow over the top of the water that stretched out gently to point straight at Oliver and Charlie.

"This is it," said Oliver, as they pulled into the driveway of a medium size house with a garage and two other cars in the driveway. "We made it."

"Holy shit. Fuck. Fuck fuck fuck," said Charlie. "This is really happening."

"Pull it together Charlie. I need you to be cool."

"I'm just going to sit in the car."

"No, you're going to have to do this with me, Charlie."

"I don't have to do shit."

"They might have seen us pull in. If only one guy comes in they may think that something is up," said Oliver. "Besides, I need you on this one. I already feel like I might piss my pants. Please, Charlie, we came all this way, just see this through with me."

"Alright, let's do this," said Charlie. "Remember, I'm Kent and you're Jeb."

"I thought you were Clark?" said Oliver.

"Yeah, Clark," said Charlie.

They stepped out of the car, and Oliver grabbed the bag. The ocean in the distance played an earthy rhythm on the background of the night air. The air smelled of the sea and just a faint hint of something that might be incense or skunk far off in the distance.

Oliver knocked on the door. "Knock, knock, knock."

"Why the fuck are you knocking like a cop?" a voice yelled from the inside.

"Why are you knocking like a cop?" whispered Charlie.

"I don't know? How does a cop knock?" asked Oliver.

They heard footsteps from within coming to the door. The door opened and a man in his late 20's with tan skin, maybe Native American maybe, Mexican answered the door.

"Yeah, what's up," said the man.

"Ah, we're here for Big Roy," said Oliver.

"Who's Big Roy?" said the man.

"I don't know. This is the address I got," said Oliver.

"You don't know who Big Roy is either?" said the man.

"Does Jackson live here?" asked Oliver.

"Who are you?" said the man.

"Jeb," said Oliver. "And this is my friend Kent."

"Come in and sit over there on the couch," said the man, pointing to a large tan sectional couch.

"Here, this is for Jackson," said Oliver, handing the man the bag.

"Why the fuck are you giving that bag to me if it's for Jackson? Did I say my name was Jackson?"

"No, is Jackson," Oliver started to say, as the man cut him off.

"Just give me the bag," said the man, taking the bag out of Oliver's hand and pointing to the couch, as he headed down the hall and into the back.

The house was dimly lit and had a resiny smell. In front of the couch was a large square coffee table. Beside the coffee table was a large, maybe 4 foot tall glass bong. On the coffee table was a Penthouse magazine, five neatly rolled neatly ordered joints, a lighter, an ashtray and a quart jar of very large buds.

"I thought my name was Clark?" whispered Charlie.

"I blanked I guess," whispered Oliver.

"Why did you give that dude the bag?" said Charlie. "What if they rob us and throw us in the ocean? Let's get the fuck out of here."

"No way, we're not going anywhere," said Oliver.

"Where did you get all the balls?" said Charlie. "What do you think the odds are we won't make it out alive? Did you see that guy? He wasn't messing around. He had that look in his eye."

"We can't leave Charlie, they have the bag. This is the address. This is where Jeb told us to go. Once we meet Jackson this will all get worked out."

Just then another man in his late twenties walked out of the hallway wearing a hat that looked like something out of the revolutionary war, black and pointing out from the sides of his head. He was also carrying a sword that looked like it came straight out of a ninja movie.

He walked into the living room, jumped up on the edge of the couch, leaped over to where Oliver was sitting, and stood straddling over top of him.

He raised the sword in the air and said, "Who the fuck are you?"

Oliver stammered, but couldn't find words.

"I will ask again," said the man quietly. "Who the fuck are you?" now a little louder.

"I'm Clark," blurted Charlie.

"I thought you were Kent," said the darker man, now suddenly in the room. Or was he there the whole time?

In the distance, the momentary silence was disturbed only by what sounded like a shower, turning off.

"I'm going to ask one more fucking time," the man said, now shouting, "who the fuck are you? And why did you come into my house carrying a bag of money with blood all over it? Answer me, or I'll chop your fucking head off!"

Just then a young woman stepped from the hallway. She had dark skin. She had a white towel around her waist and another towel in her hand that she was working on drying her dark hair with. She was naked from the waist up.

"Get down Jackson," she said calmly, still tussling her hair with the towel. You made the kid pee himself. Are you going to clean that couch?"

Oliver looked down in horror to realize that there was a large wet spot all over the front of his pants. Through all of the swelling of emotion building up inside him, the feeling that surprised him the most, was love.

"These fucking kids came into my house at 11 o'clock, on whatever the fuck day this is..."

"Sunday," Charlie interrupted.

"Shut up," said Oliver to Charlie.

"Yeah, Sunday night," said Jackson. "With a bag full of bloody money and something is up, I want to know who the fuck they are," Jackson said, stepping down from the couch wagging the sword back and forth between Oliver and Charlie. "The tall skinny one here seems like he's the ring leader."

The woman walked over and sat down on the couch next to Oliver. She picked up a joint from the table, lit it and passed it to Jackson. Jackson sat down cross legged on the coffee table and took a large puff, handing it to the darker skinned man.

"This one here," said the darker skinned man, "said his name is Jeb. This one here is either Clark or Kent."

"We are here for Big Roy," said Oliver.

"Big Roy," repeated Jackson. "I know a Jeb, and I know a Big Roy, but I don't know you. You certainly are not the Jeb I know as Big Roy," said Jackson, passing the joint to the woman.

"My name is Mia," she said, wrapping the towel she had been using to dry her hair around her breasts.

"I'm Oliver, Jeb is my brother."

"And who is your little friend over there?"

"I, I'm Charlie."

Mia motioned to hand the joint to Oliver.

"No thanks, I need to think straight."

Charlie grabbed the joint, took three large puffs in quick succession and began to cough.

"If you cough you get off," Jackson said smiling, for the first time, and relieving Charlie of the joint.

"So, where were we," said Jackson. "You are Oliver, and you are Charlie. You are here for Big Roy. You have a bag full of bloody money."

"I got a bloody nose," said Charlie.

"I thought you cleaned that up," said Oliver.

"I did the best I could. We were in the car. I didn't have much to work with."

"You stay right there," said Jackson, pointing the sword at Oliver and Charlie. "I need to make a phone call."

Jackson walked down the hallway and into a room in the back of the house.

∞

"Jeb you fuck stick. I ran into a couple of little dick beaters. You know anything about that?" said Jackson.

"A couple. I know of one," said Jeb.

"One claimed to be your little brother," said Jackson.

"That little fuck, I knew it. Was the other one short and chunky?"

"Yeah," said Jackson.

"Son of a bitch," said Jeb. "How were they doing?"

"About as well as a politician who just got caught fucking a goat in the ass, trying to explain it to his wife before the press breaks the news."

"Can you work with this?" said Jeb.

"You owe me fuck wad," said Jackson.

"Just keep them there for a few days and straighten them out before you send them back this way."

"You trust them?" said Jackson.

"Oliver is a smart kid," said Jeb. "The other one isn't so smart, but the two of them have always been close so that should be a good thing. I'll let you make the judgment call."

"Big Roy?" said Jackson. "That's the shit you wanted me to call you when we lived back in Oregon. All right Big Roy. I got this, but you owe me big."

"I'll get you back brother. Go easy on them, but make sure their head is in the game before you send them back," said Jeb.

∞

Jackson walked back into the living room.

"Alright kids," said Jackson. "I made a phone call. Everything is cool. For now."

"I just need the stuff we came for and we will leave," said Oliver.

"No can do, son," said Jackson. "Look at this grocery list we got here. You think I just keep all this shit on hand? I'm going to have to do some diving into the heart of Humboldt for this order."

"I just need to get it and go. How long is it supposed to take?" said Oliver.

"Suppose to, is relevant only to the conventional time frame of a perceived notion of how long it should take," said Jackson, taking his cross legged position back on the coffee table, and lighting another joint.

"How long is it going to take," said Oliver. "I have things to do back home."

"It's hard to say," said Jackson. "A day, maybe two, maybe five?"

"What are we going to do till then?" said Oliver.

"You're going to stay here," said Jackson. "Your brother and I go back a long way. Mi casa es su casa. Enough of this shit for now. All this bullshit is going to fuck up my circadian rhythm. If I don't get to bed soon my yoga will be shit in the morning."

"Where do we sleep then?" said Oliver.

"Chewy, can you help these kids out?" said Jackson."

"This way kids," said the man who had been sitting on the other end of the couch watching the events transpire.

"I'm Chewy," he said leading them back to a bedroom down the long hallway. "Hope you guys don't mind bunking together."

"I think we'll be okay," said Oliver.

"Jackson does yoga," snickered Charlie.

"What?" said Chewy.

"He gets weird when he smokes pot," said Oliver.

"No worries," said Chewy. "I bet he's weird without it."

"That's true. Hey, aha..." said Oliver, just realizing he had pissed himself. "Where can I clean up and change?"

"Did you guys bring stuff?" asked Chewy. "Go grab whatever you need out of your van. There is a bathroom attached to your room."

"Thanks Chewy," said Oliver.

"See you guys in the morning," said Chewy turning and entering another room in the hallway.

Oliver grabbed his things from the van and took a long hot shower. He climbed into the king size bed.

"Hey Charlie, you still awake?"

"A little, why?"

"What do you think he meant when he said 'You aren't the Jeb I know as Big Roy?'"

"That Jeb is Big Roy. He had a fucking sword. That was some cool shit," said Charlie.

"I don't get it," said Oliver.

"What's not to get," said Charlie. "Go to bed man. Everything is cool."

10

Oliver woke in the morning to a bed all by himself. The smell of bacon and eggs was in the air.

He stretched, got up and walked in the direction of the smell.

"Good morning, sunshine," said Jackson. "Easy over or sunny side up?"

"I don't really eat eggs," said Oliver, still wiping the sleepy dust out of his eyes.

"Your loss kid. These things are farm fresh. There's bacon over on the counter if you eat that."

"What's with the hat," said Oliver.

"It's a bicorne hat. This hat was actually worn by a general in Napoleons army during the battle of Waterloo in 1815. I picked it up on a backpacking trip to Europe. It cost $18,000."

"What? Who spends $18,000 on a hat, then wears it around the house?"

"What else am I going to do with the money," said Jackson. "If I spend it on shit that Uncle Sam cares about like cars and houses, I would bring unwanted attention. Besides, it's a killer hat."

Just then Charlie and Chewy walked in through the sliding glass door in the kitchen.

"You gotta check out that view Oliver," said Charlie, "It's way bigger than the Mississippi. You would need a hell of a bridge to cross that thing."

"Yeah, I'll check it out. So Jackson, what are the chances we can get what we came for and get out of here today," said Oliver.

"You're a bit uptight, aren't you son."

"I'm not a big fan of you calling me son," said Oliver. "Besides, you can't be more than a few years older than me."

"Age is a man-made dilemma. It's a measurement based on the length of time you've been breathing air and contributing to the mass hysteria we call our society. But in people years, I'm 27," said Jackson. "In answer to your question as to will you get what you came here for today? No, it won't be ready yet."

"What the fuck are we supposed to do?" said Oliver. "I have to get back and get my things ready for college. It's my senior year. I start two weeks from today. I need to take care of things. I can't be messing around on a wild goose chase looking for some funny name brand weed. I don't care what kind you give me. Just put it in a bag and I will take it back."

"Is he always like this?" Jackson asked Charlie.

"Pretty much," said Charlie. "He's always a dick in the morning."

"Fuck off Charlie," said Oliver.

"It's harvest season," said Jackson. "The trimmers are coming in tonight. You guys can join them if you want," Jackson said picking a joint out of the ashtray next to the stove and taking a pull. "Make a few bucks for your trip back."

"I'm in," said Charlie.

Just then the Mia walked in from the outside.

"Mia. My beauty," said Jackson. "This boy is up his ass in self-loathing. Would you take him for a walk and give him some ocean side medicine."

"Good morning Oliver," said Mia. "How did you sleep?"

"Like a rock," said Oliver.

"Have you seen the ocean yet?" said Mia.

Oliver and Mia walked outside the door, down the driveway and across the street. They were about 50 feet above the ocean, and took a foot path that led to the beach. At the bottom the sand was rocky and gray. Not exactly what Oliver had expected. The ocean spread from side to side and as far as the eye could see in front of him until it curved in the distance. The waves gently washed against the shore in a rhythmic, whoosh, whoosh, whoosh. A gentle breeze blew from the water and smelled of ocean air and salt and just a whiff of dead fish.

Oliver spoke first. "Is Jackson your boyfriend?"

"I guess you could call him that," said Mia.

"I just don't see someone like you with, well, someone like that," said Oliver.

"There is more to Jack than you are seeing," laughed Mia. "He can come on strong."

"He's an asshole," said Oliver.

"We've been together since high school," said Mia. "He has a way about him for sure. We are all more than one thing. He can, yes, at times be an ass hole, but he is always his true self. That's what I've always liked about him I guess."

"Who is that Chewy guy," asked Oliver.

"He grew up with us too. He's been Jack's best friend since middle school. He came from a rough home life. His parents weren't around much. Jack's family pretty much raised him. They grew up as brothers."

"Where are you guys from," said Oliver.

"Jack and Chewy are from Texas. I grew up in a military family my dad was in the Air Force, so we moved around every couple of years. My junior year we landed in San Antonio and that's where I met Jack. When it was time for me to go to college, I went to Berkley. Jack and Chewy came too. What about you? How long have you known Charlie?"

They walked north on the beach as the sun slowly rose in the sky and warmed the sand below their feet.

"We've been friends since first grade I guess. We grew up in La Crosse, Wisconsin. I've never been past Minnesota. This is the first time I've actually seen the ocean. It's different than I expected."

"What did you expect?" asked Mia.

"I guess I expected it to be more blue, and the sand to be whiter. So it doesn't seem like Chewy talks much?"

"He has never been burdened with the need to say more than what he has to. Most people feel obligated to say things or make small talk to make themselves feel comfortable in social situations. We are doing it right now. Some people just talk to hear themselves speak. Chewy has never been like that. I have learned that if Chewy says something, it is worth paying attention."

"I'm not talking to make myself comfortable. I like talking to you," said Oliver.

"It's okay," said Mia. "Let's just walk for a while. You can learn a lot about a place, and a person by walking without words."

They walked, and the beach became a narrow spit of land, the big lagoon on one side and the ocean on the other. Seagulls circled and landed on the beach in front of them. As they got closer, the seagulls rose up, circled and landed further down the beach. They walked slowly, then sat for a while, and walked some more. After about an hour Oliver turned and they started walking back.

"Jackson said the trimmers were coming tonight," said Oliver. "Who are the trimmers?"

"It's harvest season. The trimmers come in to help trim the buds. When the plants grow they produce leaves and flowers. The flowers are the buds. That is the part that can be smoked. The leaves have to be trimmed off. That's what the trimmers do. Who are they? They are a bunch of kids from all over. It's always great having them. You'll see."

"Do you have any idea how long it's going to take Jackson to get what we came here for?" asked Oliver.

"When everything is ready," said Mia. "Look, that's the path that leads back to the house."

11

The first one to arrive was named Jason, a tall, skinny, back to the earth type hippie who lived in a yurt that he built somewhere in the hills of Siskiyou County. In the early afternoon Star and Megan showed up from Bend, Oregon. Rex and Sam, friends of Mia's from Berkley came in around 3 P.M.

Jackson came out of the garage with a large black garbage bag, bulging at the sides and set it down next to the large table everyone was gathered around.

"Here is the beginning guys," said Jackson, "dig in."

Everyone began to dig in, except Oliver who sat and watched.

"What am I supposed to do with these?" said Charlie.

"Take a branch like this one," said Star. "Here are the buds. Start by clipping these off and throw the branch in the garbage. Take each bud and trim all the leaves that poke out the sides, like this. Don't go to deep. You want it to look kind of like this when you're done." She held up a neatly trimmed cone shaped bud. "Then you put it in your pile."

"You guys need anything," said Mia. "Beer, tea, water? Jackson's going to be starting the grill in a little while if anyone is hungry."

"Spark one up," said Megan.

"So what's your story," said Star to Oliver. "I've never seen you around here."

"I'm from Wisconsin," said Oliver, still sitting in his chair looking around unsure what to do.

"No way," said Star. "Megan is from Wisconsin. Aren't you Megan?"

"Yeah, Green Bay," said Megan, taking a large pull from a freshly rolled joint. "Is your friend here from Wisconsin too?"

"We're from La Crosse," added Charlie.

"I grew up on the coast," said Star. "My parents did a lot of bouncing around, but we always stayed near the coast. My dad is a surfer. Now they have a little ranch here in southern Humboldt. They have a great crop this year."

"I'm not feeling very good," said Oliver, standing up and walking towards the door. He stepped outside and felt the cool ocean breeze hit his face. There was a little cement patio with two chairs and a small table. He sat down. The sun was high in the sky still, but casting down towards the water. A small group of seagulls were riding thermals of air cast up by the ridge-line separating the top of the bank from the beach 50 feet below.

Chewy stepped out on the patio and joined him. "Hello Oliver."

"Hi," said Oliver.

"You mind if I sit down," said Chewy.

"It's not my house," said Oliver.

"If it were you're house, would you mind if I sat down?"

"No, I'm sorry, that's not what I meant."

Chewy sat down. "I really like sitting out here. Especially, as the sun is going down. There is this split second as the sun fades into the water. The very last sliver of sun. Just for a second it shines infinitely bright. Then pssst... it gets snuffed out by the water."

"I've never been to the ocean before," said Oliver.

"How do you like it?" asked Chewy.

"I don't even like weed," said Oliver, changing the subject, "it makes me paranoid."

"Why are you here?" asked Chewy.

"I don't know. My brother asked me to do this thing. I felt obligated I guess."

"I can understand that feeling of obligation," said Chewy. "That's what brothers do for each other."

"This is just so. So fucked up," said Oliver, burying his face in his hands.

"Are you afraid?"

"Of course I'm afraid," said Oliver. "They could put me in a cage. I could be locked in a cage and my life would be over."

"You don't have to do this, you know that right," said Chewy.

"Yes I do," said Oliver.

"When we were kids," said Chewy, "there was a high dive at our school. Most kids couldn't even get themselves to dive off it. Jackson and I started diving. Then we started doing flips. Pretty soon I was doing one and a halves. I realized that when I was in the air I still had a little time left in my rotation, so I started doing double front flips. For a while I was landing them every time. One right after another. Until one time, just as I was leaving the end of the diving board I heard Jackson yell. 'You're not going to make it.' For some reason I froze. I rotated a little, and came down like a brick straight on my back. It hurt. Bad. I got back up and got back onto the diving board. Did my usual run up to the end of the board. Hit the end, flailed a little and smash, right on my back again. I was frozen by the fear. Something that I had done multiple times in a row suddenly seemed out of reach for me."

"Did you ever do it again?" said Oliver. "The double?"

"I learned something about fear that day. I learned that it can blind you."

There was a long pause. Chewy got up and opened the door to go into the house.

"Thanks Chewy," said Oliver.

"Everyone has fear Oliver," said Chewy, as he walked in the door.

"Oliver, look at this plate of steaks," said Jackson walking out the door with a large plate piled high with steaks. "I buy half a cow every couple of months from a farmer just south of Eureka. Free range and all that shit. These are the best quality steaks in Humboldt. Almost as good as the ones we grew up with in Texas. You do eat steaks right?"

"Yeah, I eat steaks," said Oliver.

"Around here you have to ask," said Jackson. "At least you can cook steaks up here. When we were down in Berkley you fire up a grill and put some steaks on and you've got a protest in your front yard. I could really give two shits about people having a fit about my steaks, but they're not as open down there about the weed thing as they are up here. It wasn't like Texas or anything, but who needs the extra attention."

"How long have you been growing weed?" said Oliver.

"I started growing it in Berkley. I've been dealing it since I was 14. My dad was the high school football coach, so I knew all the older guys."

"Mia said you went to college at Berkley with her. What did you study?"

"I studied how to grow weed," laughed Jackson. "Mia went to school. Chewy and I shared a house with her. I did take a few classes here and there, mainly to keep my parents off my case, but I never prescribed to the whole organized education thing. It seems too much like a religion to me. You've got one person standing on a pulpit, preaching to class about one subject and they never change message. Then they test you to see if you memorized all the shit they want you to remember. A few hundred years ago they were teaching that the world was flat. If you would have answered that you thought the world was round and not the center of the universe, but in fact traveling around the sun you would have answered wrong. Then you have history, which is completely fucked. His story is always the one made up by whoever won. Aren't you in college? What do you study?"

"English," said Oliver. "I'm a writer. Well, I want to be."

"I want to be a fucking pirate, so that's what I am," said Jackson. "You are what you want to be, son. If you're not then you're not anything, and you get sucked into his story."

"I'm just saying I've never really written anything yet."

"Never? I bet they make you write all kinds of shit in that school you go to," said Jackson.

"I mean I've never had anything published. The biggest thing I've ever been published in is the school paper, but that doesn't really count."

"So no one has ever told you you're good enough to be a writer? You haven't written a New York Times best seller yet? No one has read your work?"

"Well no one has paid me for anything," said Oliver.

"Here," said Jackson, reaching into his wallet, "here is a $100 bill. Write me a story some time. This one hundred dollars is going to make you a writer."

"Thanks, but I don't have time for games," said Oliver. "I have to get back to the real world."

"What do you think is happening here? This is as real as it gets."

"You know what I mean. I can't stick around here. I really have to get back."

"Things take time Oliver. You are free to go back to 'the real world' any time you like."

"Sorry, I'm not trying to offend you. Of course it's real here. I meant..."

"I know what you meant," said Jackson. "I don't get offended. Unless you come into my house at 11 o'clock at night with a bag full of bloody money."

"You got me there," said Oliver.

"These steaks are done. Help me carry them in."

"Hey Oliver," said Charlie, as Oliver came through the door. "Look at this pile. I've probably made $100 already."

12

Oliver and Charlie sat by themselves on a little patio behind the house, as the rest of the trimmers ate inside.

"So Oliver," said Charlie, "are you going to trim at all?"

"I'm not sure," said Oliver.

"You could use the money as much, or more than I could," said Charlie.

"My head's not really into it. I just keep thinking about everything. We've got to get back."

"I kind of like it here. Did you see that girl Megan? The one from Wisconsin?"

"Of course I did," said Oliver.

"She's hot," said Charlie. "I think she likes me. She keeps talking to me. Asking questions."

"Questions about what?"

"You know the usual stuff. Where I'm from. What I do. Why we're here."

"What the fuck Charlie. What did you tell here we're here for? You want the whole world to know."

"Who is she going to tell? She's been sitting next to me trimming weed. You think she cares?"

"Not everyone needs to know what we are doing Charlie. When we get home you better not tell anyone. If it gets back to my mom that I was driving weed across the country she would never get over it. You can't tell anyone when we get back. Do you hear me?"

"Yeah, yes, I hear you," said Charlie.

"I'm serious Charlie. You can't go around bragging about this."

"I got it," said Charlie. "Oliver, you have to relax a little bit. We are in a really cool place. We're stuck here so you might as well enjoy it. Smoke a little weed."

"No Charlie. That isn't going to help anything. When I smoke weed I think the world is out to get me. Like everything is conspiring against me."

"What's the difference between then and the rest of the time," laughed Charlie.

"Honestly, I don't know."

"You're so fucking serious all the time," said Charlie. "You're going to have a heart attack or something."

The back sliding door opened and Mia poked her head out. "We're all going down to the beach to watch the sunset. Come on guys. You're coming too."

"You heard her," said Charlie. "We're going too."

"Yeah, I'm coming."

"You need to stop being such a buzz kill man. You deserve a little vacation. Enjoy this."

"I don't need to smoke weed to enjoy this," said Oliver.

"Smoke weed. Don't smoke weed. Who cares? Just get out of your head man. I'm here too. I'm your best friend. In a couple of weeks you're going to go back to school and I'm going to be all alone again. Let's hang out. Let's have fun."

"It's not that easy," said Oliver.

"Come on," said Charlie. "They're headed down right now."

Oliver and Charlie were the last ones to leave the house. By the time they got outside the front door all they could see of the others was Jason, the new age hippie, headed over the edge of the drop off to the shore. The sun was about two fingers above the multicolored skyline, and descending.

When they reached the beach everyone was there. Two blankets were spread on the ground, one blue and one red. A couple of joints were being passed around.

"Come sit," said Mia.

Oliver and Charlie sat on the red blanket with Mia, Star and Megan.

"Have you met Star and Megan, Oliver?" said Mia.

"Yeah, I met them earlier when they first got here."

"Hi Oliver," said Star.

"Hello," said Oliver.

"Charlie said you're going back to school in a couple of weeks. What are you going to school for? What's your major?" asked Star.

"I'm an English major," said Oliver.

"What is your favorite book?" asked Star.

"I'm not sure. There are so many good books. I think my favorite author is Steinbeck, probably East of Eden I guess."

"Do you want some of this," Star reached out and passed the joint to Oliver.

"Sure," Oliver said. He took a long pull, inhaling it all the way down, and began to cough. "I don't normally smoke," Oliver said when his coughing had stopped, and passed the joint to Charlie, who was talking to Megan.

"I don't smoke much either," said Star. "I don't know how these guys around here do it. I can't smoke every day and enjoy it."

"They smoke too much," said Mia. "I smoke too much sometimes too."

"You seem fine," said Oliver.

"I am fine," said Mia. "If I take some time away from smoking and come back to it I feel better. Jackson can smoke all day every day and never seem to stray from who he is. If I smoke like that I start to get cloudy. I start to feel a little numb."

"It makes me feel paranoid," said Oliver, taking another drag of the joint as it came back around.

"I think too much about myself sometimes," said Star. "Sometimes I have to play a game with myself I call, 'there are other people too.' It sounds stupid, but I just think to myself about other people. I tell myself that I'm not the only one here. I think it's kind of selfish to feel sorry for myself. Do you know what I mean?"

"I think so," said Oliver.

"Everyone has a different path, and everyone sees the world through a different lens," said Mia. "When marijuana comes on, she accesses different pathways in your brain. It's easy to feel self-conscious about that. It's easy to get caught in patterns, also. Like the story of Pavlov and his bell. Every time the bell rang the dogs would salivate. Every time you smoke you get that self-conscious feeling. The breakthroughs in life happen when we move beyond the patterns. That's what I like about this herb. It gives me opportunities to shift my thought patterns."

The sun drifting towards the horizon. Big orange ball just about to touch the surface of the water. Laughter rang from the beach and faded into the washing waves. Whoosh, whoosh, whoooshhhh, whoosh...

The big orange ball seemed to move faster now that it had landed on the horizon. Slipping into the depths. Orange to pink to red. Halfway submerged. Rippling spectrals of evaporation like waves coming off a hot paved road echoed off the water as the sun sank. Slowly, yet slipping.

A crest of orange red on top of the distant ocean. It's passing almost somber. Like the loss of something. A dream maybe that was once there and will come again, but never in the same way.

The last little sliver slid down, down faster and faster. In the last moment, as the rotation gave it its final nudge, a light shot from the surface of the water. A beam. A white star candle. Whisp...and it was extinguished. Leaving an orange glow over a black ocean with no horizon. The water and the sky collapse into one another.

Blackness slowly creeped skyward. The ocean swallowed the sky and there was no stratification of the two. They had merged. The light was no more. Only black.

Blink. Blink. Blink. A light blinked far out in the ocean. As far out as can be seen on the bend of the earth. Blink. Blink. Blink. A ship sailed from somewhere to somewhere else. Floating, drifting alone. Behind it the stars slowly begin to emerge from the night.

"Does body have a flashlight?" yelled Charlie.

"We don't need a flashlight," yelled Jackson. "What we need is to empty our lungs. Fuck you ocean! You won't take me alive!"

"Fuck you moon," yelled Megan, "we don't need you tonight!"

"Fuck you world! I'm in California!" shouted Charlie.

"Fuck you sun! We don't need you anymore today!" screamed Star.

"Fuck you Jeb, you piece of shit! Fuck you I hate you!" said Oliver.

"Yeah, fuck you Jeb!" yelled Jackson. "Get it out kid. Let the ocean hear your troubles! It will suck them into its moon pull. The tides of summer are going away and they take all your screams with them."

"AAAAhHhhhhh... I love you mom, but I hate your cancer! Go away!" screamed Oliver. "I want to go home."

Whoosh. Whhhhooosshh. Whosh. Whoosh...said the waves.

"All right fuckers. Play time is over," said Jackson. "Let's get back to work."

The party silently walked up the beach and the path leading to the house. Their eyes could see the ground in front of them just enough to navigate the trail. A slight glow emanated from the houses along the street above. Oliver wondered how his eyes would do in complete darkness. Would his feet be able to sense the path and lead him home?

They rose to the top of the small cliff and crossed the empty road back to the house in silence.

"Does your mom really have cancer?" asked Charlie as they got close to the house. "Why didn't you tell me?"

"I didn't really want to talk about it. I don't really want to talk about it."

Everyone sat back down in their places, talking and laughing. Telling stories of life.

"Who wants a beer," said Jackson, grabbing a few Mad River beers from the fridge and passing them out amongst the workers.

"This job is awesome," said Charlie.

"That's why we come down here," said Megan.

'Reservoir Dogs' played on the television and Oliver sank into the couch.

"Oliver, I'm going to town," said Mia. "Do you want to come with?"

"No," said Oliver.

"You can sit here all by yourself, or you can sit in my car all by yourself it's up to you," she said. "We don't even have to talk. It would be good for you to have some human interaction."

The TV was playing a little too loud, so the people in the back of the room at the table could hear it. Oliver felt cradled in the couch. He forced himself to sit up.

"I'll go," he said.

The car pulled out of the driveway and onto Highway 101. No one spoke.

They pulled off at the Arcata exit and made their way into town, pulling into the Peoples Food Co-op. Oliver had been into a few food co-ops in La Crosse and Madison, Wisconsin. He wondered how all of them could smell the same. That mild perfume, mixed with produce and a slight whiff of hippie.

This co-op was a little different though, because it seemed that everyone here, with the exception of himself, seemed hippie, like they were all drinking the same Kool-Aid. Dreadlocks and wispy beards, patterned sweatshirts and lots of people carrying what looked to be handmade bags. Almost all of them pretty close to his age or a few years older. He felt as though he may have somehow been transported to a different place or time.

Mia picked up a few things, mostly food for the guests. They paid and went out to the parking lot.

"Let's drop this stuff in the car for now and walk into town a little bit. I have to say hi to a friend at a coffee shop down town," said Mia.

They walked down the dark lamp lit street that seemed to be buzzing with activity for being a Monday night.

"Mia, how are you."

"I am well. Hello Alex and Wendy," said Mia.

"Are you going to the mountain Friday night?" asked the girl.

"We will be there," said Mia. "Alex, Wendy, this is Oliver."

"Hello," said Oliver, breaking his silence for the first time.

They walked on, down a hill towards the city center.

"It seems different here," said Oliver.

"Different how?" said Mia.

"I don't know. Different like everyone dresses different than I'm used to I guess. I get a feeling that everyone acts different too."

"This is a college town," said Mia. "HSU is just over there, on the other side of the 101."

"I go to school in Madison, WI. It's a college town and it's pretty liberal. This just feels somehow, like something more."

"I do know what you mean," said Mia. "I often feel like it has something to do with the redwoods, but I think it's more to do with the way that the people who settled here in the last half century have carried traditions on. I think it's a movement that was started in the sixties and it's just so inviting that the youth here have embraced it and carried it out and kept its spirit alive."

"Like how?" asked Oliver.

"In the sixties lots of people flocked to the west coast during the original hippie movement. Many of them moved to the bay area or other more southern cities. During the 70's there were so many people here that the prices along the coast skyrocketed.

Around the same time, up here in northern California, the lumber industry, which had been booming for the first part of the century, was screeching to a halt. The redwood curtain was being pulled down and forestry was almost halted in the name of saving what remained of the redwood forests. Lumber workers were not happy.

Many of the small towns in the area pretty much turned into ghost towns, almost overnight. The lumber workers began moving out and the hippies from the lower part of the state, the artist and activists began moving in and creating their own communities. At first the locals didn't want them here, but they helped support the local economy."

"Is that who started the weed growing culture here?" asked Oliver.

"Yeah, it started pretty small at first, just the newcomers growing a little for personal use, but there are so many back woods in these areas it was easy to slowly scale up. Since the lumber industry, which was the primary industry for the first part of the century, had dried up so quickly the economy was in need of another cash crop. The artists and the hippies did bring the weed to the area, for the most part, but after seeing the potential of marijuana as a cash crop, even the locals began embracing and welcoming the new industry. One thing to remember about the people who originally settled these lands is that many of them were already outlaws. They came to the coast looking for gold and ultimately stayed because they wanted to be as far as possible from the heavy hand of the law. As far as possible from the east. There are many places in this area that never stopped serving whiskey during the alcohol prohibition of the 1920's. It was a point of pride for the locals, and a sign of their independence. By the mid 1980's marijuana had become the main cash crop in the region."

They came to a small coffee shop at the end of the town square, and went inside. Mia greeted several people, and introduced Oliver.

"Oliver, this is Jacob and Marry," said Mia. "Do you want a coffee?"

"Sure," said Oliver. "No cream or sugar."

"Stay here," said Mia. "I'll be back in a few minutes."

"Where are you from," said the girl introduced as Marry.

Mia stepped behind the counter, greeted the barista and entered a room behind the counter.

"What, oh, I'm ah, I'm from Wisconsin," said Oliver.

"Cool," said Marry. "Jacob is from Michigan. That's right by Wisconsin, isn't it? I'm from Washington State. We both came here for school. How do you know Mia? We met her at a bonfire on the beach. She's a pretty special person. It's like she knows things. It's really weird. You know...in a good way. Sometimes when I'm talking to her it feels like she's looking right inside of me. But it's not scary."

Just then Mia reappeared from the back room and rejoined the small group.

"Thank you for keeping Oliver company," said Mia.

"No problem," said Marry.

"He's cute," said Jacob.

"Stay away from this one, Jacob," laughed Mia.

"Are you going to be at the Mountain Friday night?" asked Marry.

"We will be there," said Mia.

With that they walked back out onto the dimly lit sidewalk.

13

Oliver woke to a full bed. Star and Megan had also shared a bed with them. Everyone was fully clothed, though Megan and Charlie were huddled together. Oliver woke up with Star's arm resting on his shoulder. She still seemed to be asleep.

He walked sleepy eyed into the living room. The air smelled deeply of the rich dank tones of marijuana mixed with a slight ocean texture that only someone who didn't live on the coast would notice.

∞

"Mom," Oliver said into his cell phone.

"Oliver, how are you?" said his mother.

"I'm good Mom. Just wanted to call to see how you are doing."

"I'm fine Oliver. How is your trip?"

"My trip is going good." Oliver sat down in a chair on the front patio. The sun was just on its way up. Looking out he saw a long pink streak in the sky over the deep blue ocean.

"How long are you going to stay there? You know you have to get back to school right?"

"Yeah Ma, I know. Just a few more days and we're going to head back."

"A few more days? A few more days! You have responsibilities here Oliver. You know I'm sick Oliver."

"I have things I need to do here too Mom."

"Things? What things? Like chase little girls around and do drugs. Are you doing drugs Oliver? Are you hooked on drugs?"

"No Mom I'm not hooked on drugs."

"I heard about that crystal meth business all the kids are into these days. It will ruin your life Oliver."

"I'm not doing crystal meth mom. That shit is nasty."

"Don't swear at me Oliver, and good. That stuff makes your teeth fall out and puts holes in your brain. Your brain will look like Swiss cheese."

"I swear Mom. I would never touch that stuff."

"Good. How is Charlie? Is he keeping you out of trouble? He's probably the only one with a level head out there. That Charlie is a good boy. Can I talk to him?"

"No Mom, he's still sleeping."

"He's still sleeping. It's 10 o'clock in the morning."

"It's only 8 o'clock here Mom, there's a time difference."

"Oh Oliver. It scares me for you to be so far away. What if something happens to you? I won't be able to help. I won't be able to do anything."

"Don't worry about me Mom. How are you? Have you been to the doctor since I left?"

"Yeah, I went."

"What did they say?"

"You know. They said what they always say. Blahh blahh... You have cancer. We have to start treatment soon. Blahh blahh... There is a chance of recovery if you, blahh blahh..."

"If you what Mom? A chance of recovery if you what?"

"If I do chemo therapy."

"So when do you start."

"I don't know Oliver. You don't need to worry about this stuff. You have your own life to live. You have a long life ahead of you."

"What is that supposed to mean. You're not going to take the treatment?"

"Oh, I don't know. I know people who have gone through it. It sounds terrible. You lose all your hair. What do I have if I don't have my hair, Oliver?"

"You have life Mom. You have us. Me and Jeb."

"You boys don't need me anymore. I did my work with you. I worked hard. I gave you everything I had. What is life Oliver?"

"What do you mean, what is life?"

"I mean, what does it mean Oliver? What does life mean? What does it mean to be alive? What would it mean if I weren't here anymore? You would be sad for a while. Jeb would feel guilty for a while. What would I be?"

"Don't talk like that Mom. You are going to take the chemo therapy and get better. Everything is going to be fine."

"What is life for Oliver? Why are we here? I want you to answer that for me Oliver. You have always been a smart boy. I want you to think about that."

"Life is about hard choices. You always told me that. It sounds to me like you're giving up."

"I've got to go Oliver. I'm running late for my hair appointment. That Tracy is a real bitch if you mess up her schedule. I don't trust her with my hair when she's angry."

"Wait. Mom..."

"Got to go Oliver. I love you. Be good. Tell Charlie I said Hello. Come home soon."

"Love you too, Mom. Wait."

Click.

∞

"But Mom," Oliver found himself saying out loud, "I don't know what life is about. I don't know why we're here."

He sat there, alone for a long time. Looking out at the waves. Wondering. Why are we here? What the fuck do we have to live for?

The seagulls gathered over the edge of the drop off, riding the air currents at the top of the ridge. It looked like 10 of them. Wait was there 9 or 11? They bobbed, they swirled, but they never stood still long enough to count. They all looked the same from this distance. The wind hit Oliver's face in one steady shallow breeze.

"What's up kid?" said Jackson, setting down a plate of eggs and toast. "You eat eggs today? These come from a friend down the road. Raises them right in her yard."

"Yeah, thanks Jackson. I'll eat the eggs."

"Did you know that chickens rarely go outside of their home range? As long as you give them a house and food they will never leave. They'll wander all over your yard, but they're not going to go anywhere. Catching them once they're out of the coop is a different story. Until night time. The funny thing about night time is that when it gets close to dark, they will just roost down wherever they are and fall to sleep. You can just reach down and pick them up, they barely wake up."

"Any word on the rest of our stuff?" asked Oliver.

"Lots of words. Words don't mean much though. We get way too caught up in words, generally speaking. We get so caught up in words that we think they are what the stories we tell are made of."

"You know what I mean," said Oliver. "When can we get out of here?"

"You can leave any time you want, little brother," said Jackson.

"Stop fucking with me. You know exactly what I mean. I need the shit we came here for and I need to get home. My fucking mom is dying of cancer. I'm leaving for school in two weeks. I don't want to be here anymore. I need to get home. I need the shit we came for and I need to get the fuck out of this place!"

"Do you think she will die less with you there? We are all dying. The moment we are born we are on that path."

"She needs me. I need to be there."

"Then why the fuck did you come here? Why aren't you curled up at her feet and waiting for her to kick off?"

"What the fuck dude? Who fucking says that?" said Oliver.

"I'm just saying, kid. I haven't seen you call her since you've been here until this morning. How often do you actually spend time with her when you're at home? What's the difference if you're here or there?" said Jackson.

"How the fuck do you know? Have you been spying on me? Monitoring my phone calls?"

"Hey kid, tell yourself whatever you want. You leave here whenever you're ready. Not a minute later. I'm going to tell you now. I'm not going to have your 'shit' until it's ready. It's not ready yet. You're in a weird space in your life right now. I get that. That's why I'm cutting you so much slack," said Jackson.

"Cutting me slack?" said Oliver. "Cutting me slack? You're the biggest dick I've ever met. You almost cut my head off with a sword. You insist on calling me a kid. I don't even believe that you don't have the weed we came here for packed and ready to go. You just want to torture me, or use us so Charlie will keep trimming for you, or some shit. I don't even know. You're a douche bag."

"Ha... See? Cutting you slack. I would punch you right in the face if I didn't like you so much. Enjoy your eggs. Enjoy the view. Chewy made those eggs for you. That guy knows how to make an egg. Eggs are a very delicate food. They are so common and most people are used to eating eggs that have had the shit beat out of them. They are used to those store bought eggs with no flavor, then they put them in a pan and fry the shit out of them and add so much salt and pepper that all you taste is a flat, dry, crusty puck. Chewy knows how to handle an egg."

"What is there to enjoy? How would you know? My life is shit. I don't want to be here. My mom is dying. I have shit to do back home. I have so much shit I need to do. Why the fuck am I hear Jackson? Why?"

"You're here to eat your eggs and enjoy the view, kid. All the other shit will happen. Did you ever play hide and seek when you were a kid? We all did, I know. Pretty much every American kid who ever lived played that game. What do you say when it's time to go looking for everyone?"

"Ready or not, here I come?" said Oliver.

"Exactly. See I do know some shit about you, and that's something we both learned. Just imagine what's in there," said Jackson pointing at Oliver's heart. "The things we were born with. When you get down far enough. When you cut right down to the center. We are all the same. We are all playing hide and seek our whole lives.

"To find life you just need to keep the right mindset and everything will happen. You have to wake up every morning, no matter where you wake up, and say, 'Ready or not here I come.'"

"Dude," said Charlie, busting out onto the front patio. "Oliver, she kissed me! Last night before we went to bed she fucking kissed me. She wouldn't let me go any further, but she let me keep my hand on her boob all night when we slept. Dude, this is the best vacation ever. Oh, hey Jackson."

"Nice work killer," said Jackson. "Those Oregon girls are a lot of fun."

"What do you mean fun?" said Charlie. "You mean you've... Have you?"

"No man. I just meant fun," laughed Jackson. "They are fun to be around."

"I think she likes me," said Charlie.

"She has been diggin' on you," said Jackson.

"What do I do?"

"Well, holding her boob was good," said Jackson. "You just got to follow that up with being a little more manly."

"I can do manly," said Charlie. "You mean like holding doors and paying for stuff right?"

"Only if it seems right at the time. Just be yourself kid," said Jackson. "She's liking you for who you already are. Don't change a thing. Just be brave. That doesn't mean pushy. Just have some balls."

"What do you think, Oliver?" said Charlie.

"She seems cool," said Oliver. "Looks like she's coming out right now."

"Shhh... Don't tell her I told you guys anything," said Charlie.

"Hey guys," said Megan, walking out onto the front patio with Star. "We were going to go for a walk on the beach. You guys want to come?"

"Yeah, we'll come," said Charlie.

"I'm going to stay here," said Oliver.

"Come on, Oliver. You need to lighten up a little," said Charlie. "Come on man I need you," he whispered.

"Alright," said Oliver.

"You coming, Jackson?" said Star.

"Nope, I got chores around the homestead. You guys have fun. Catch me one of those seagulls for dinner."

The four of them walked across the street and down the path to the beach. The morning sun had brightened the sky and turned everything from the ocean out, a panorama of blues.

"So what about you mystery man," said Star. "Where have you been hiding?"

"Who me?" said Oliver.

"Yeah you. Charlie says you're his best friend, but we've barely seen you at all."

"I've been. You know. I've been around," said Oliver.

"So your mom has cancer?" said Star.

"Star... Give the man a break," said Megan.

"No, it's okay," said Oliver. "Yeah, I guess."

"That's really heavy," said Star. "My mom had breast cancer. It almost ten years ago now. It seems like it was yesterday. I was just a kid when she was diagnosed. It was super scary."

"Here, you want the first pull," said Megan, handing Oliver a neatly rolled joint.

"Yeah," said Oliver. He took the joint and pressed it between his lips. Star cupped her hands around the end of the joint and lit it. He took a long steady drag. Then another. Then another.

"Hey, slow down there chief," said Megan. "We only brought one."

Oliver passed the joint on. They walked for a while and talked. They walked in the direction of Patrick's Point this time, and found themselves on a little corner in the beach.

"Mia told me this beach is called Agate Beach," said Megan. "I guess you can find agates here. They're kind of hard to find now though, because all the tourists come and comb the beach and fill their pockets. It's crazy to think of cleaning a beach of all its stones one pocket full at a time."

"Is this an agate?" said Charlie.

"I'm not sure," said Megan.

"What about this one?" said Charlie.

"Still not sure," said Megan.

Megan and Charlie combed the beach looking for agates. Oliver drifted off towards the edge of the water looking into the distance and Star caught up with him.

"Oliver, do you know how to skip stones?" said Star.

"Yeah," said Oliver. "My brother and I used to ride our bikes down to the Mississippi river and skip stones when we were kids."

"Older brother or younger?" asked Star, picking up a smooth palm sized rock and expertly curling her finger around the edge, before bending ever so slightly to meet the angle of the water and flicking the rock... skip. Skip. Skip. Skip skip skip skip. Across the water.

"He's older. Doesn't always act older though," Oliver said bending to pick up a silver dollar sized flat stone.

"Do you have any other brothers or sisters?" said Star.

"Nope," said Oliver, launching his rock. Skip. Skip. Skid. "Just the one."

"I have a younger sister. She still lives at home. She's 17. I think I know what you mean about the doesn't seem older thing. My little sister seems a lot more mature than I did when I was her age. I rebelled a lot though. Partied and made my parents worry way too much. Shit, they were hippie pot farmers, what did I have to rebel against," said Star picking up another stone.

"I think some people just want to grow up as fast as they can. My brother never seemed like he wanted to be a kid. He always wanted to hang out with older kids and do stuff that he wasn't supposed to do. Stuff he just wasn't old enough for, like smoke cigarettes and drink. He was smoking weed when he was like 14. I was stuck at home with mom watching her flip out because she didn't know where he was."

"I smoked weed for the first time when I was 13. Not that I'm proud of it or anything. It was always around. I didn't really like it though," said Star. "I didn't really understand it like I do now. I hardly smoked at all when I was a teenager except the few times I snuck it and smoked pretty much just for the thrill of trying to not get caught. It was the drinking that my parents hated. Sometimes I would leave for days and not tell them where I was going or when I would be home. They were cool though. My mom would try and have these heart to heart talks with me and I would just tune out. I was so. So... Bad to them. My sister's not like that. She's a good student, a killer surfer and genuinely sweet. I love hanging out with her."

"Sounds like you were like my brother," said Oliver.

"Yeah, maybe," said Star. "Has anyone ever told you, you're really easy to talk to? You listen. Most guys our age just wait to speak, and are more concerned with talking about themselves. I don't get that from you. I feel like you have a lot to say, but you are considerate of others, and have a natural way of connecting."

"I don't know about that," said Oliver, feeling suddenly self-conscious and shy. "I usually have a hard time connecting with other people, especially girls. I like to listen. I never thought about it before, but I think I listen more because I have to try hard to connect with others. I think some people don't listen because they don't really care about what the people around them think. They just want to tell them what they think. And most of the time that's all anybody wants to hear."

"See, there's something about you Oliver. Something special. I'll figure it out," smiled Star. "Hey, Megan and I are going down to visit my parents at their farm tomorrow. Do you and Charlie want to come?"

"I don't know," said Oliver. "We're on kind of a tight schedule. We may have to leave at any time. Aren't you guys working for Jackson anyway?"

"It's not like he has us chained to the table," said Star. "Jackson and Mia and Chewy are cool. They don't care. Either we come and help, or we don't, leave or don't leave. What we do here is pretty much migrant work. We just get paid for what we do. I like it. It's fun to sit around and talk and smoke a little. Who else gets to work and watch movies and have great conversation? It's kind of a hobby for me."

"Do you ever worry about getting in trouble?" asked Oliver.

"No. Everybody is pretty cool around here. You're coming from the Midwest. It's like the Bible belt out there still. It's not the same here. I was Megan's first friend out here, she was pretty weirded out at first too. She got used to it though."

"Yeah, it's not the same at all," said Oliver.

"Think about it though. We're only going to be down there for like a day," said Star. "My mom makes the best vegetarian lasagna, and they love company."

"I guess we can think about it," said Oliver.

"Hey Oliver," Charlie said, running over. "Check this out. This has to be an agate for sure. Megan found it."

Charlie held up a smooth, semi-translucent orange stone with white milky bands about the size of a dime.

"This has to be an agate. Look how cool it is"

"Yeah, that's pretty cool," said Oliver.

"Whatever man," said Charlie, "be skeptical all you want. I'm going to keep this one. Hey, Megan told me that her and Star are going down to Southern Humboldt tomorrow morning."

"Yeah, I heard about it," said Oliver.

"Megan said that…"

"Charlie, you know why we're here."

"These girls are hot, Oliver, and they are inviting us to hang out with them."

"I'm standing right here," smiled Star.

"Hi Star," said Charlie. "Tell this guy how cool it would be. Tell him we could go surfing."

Megan walked up holding another stone and gave it to Charlie.

"We'll see," said Oliver. "I need to check with Jackson."

"Yes, we're in ladies," said Charlie.

14

When the group got back to the house the other trimmers had already started for the day. The house was dim and smoky. Dank streams of light poured in through the front window. Chewy was bringing a new large black plastic garbage bag of branches for the trimmers to start in on.

"Hey guys," said Mia, stretching and doing what seemed to be yoga on the living room floor under the window.

"Hey Mia," said Star.

The girls went back to the table and started in on the work for the day.

"You going to trim today?" said Charlie. "I've got almost two pounds already. That's about four hundred bucks. I know you could use the money for school too."

"I don't know. I just don't feel like sitting around a table with a bunch of people I don't know and talking to them right now," said Oliver.

"Who said you have to talk. Besides, they are all super cool. That Jason guy lives off the land and shit. He only eats meat that he kills. This is the only thing that he does that he says he 'trades his freedom for money.' Whatever that means. I think it means he never has to sit down and do anything for anyone, and that's why he's free? I don't know, but he seems really cool."

"I'll think about it."

"Fuck thinking about it. It's not hard. Besides, one of the coolest things to do when you're high is focus on one thing. Just grab some trimming scissors, take a toke and space the fuck out. Who cares," said Charlie.

"What's with the peer pressure, Charlie," said Oliver.

"I just want to hang out with you man. This is like the biggest adventure of my life and you're off on your own little 'Oliver is the saddest kid in the room' thing. I just want you to snap out of it and have a good time, that's all. I know getting back is important to you, but we are here man. We have the rest of our lives to be back there."

"All right, you got me Charlie. I'm in."

Oliver sat down at the table. He was given a small pile of branches and a pair of stout scissors with springs that opened up after each cut. "Return of the Jedi," was playing on the TV. A joint came around the table and Oliver took a drag and passed it along.

He looked around to see what everyone else was doing, picked up a branch and started by snipping off all the buds onto a plate in front of him. He picked up one of the buds and looked at it. It looked to him like some kind of alien. If he looked really close, it looked like it had little hairs, and if held in the light just the right way it looked like it had crystals all over it. There were skinny little, pointy, wavy leaves sticking out from all sides.

He'd never really looked at a bud close like this. All the ones he had seen before had been shoved in the bottom of a baggie and probably came compressed with a bunch of other similar buds all packed together. Truth be told, he had never actually owned his own bag of weed, and the few times he had smoked in the past he never even touched it. He just took the pipe and smoked what was handed to him. As he thought about it, this may have been the first time he had ever really held a true bud in his hand.

The bud itself was about the size of his thumb. He looked around and everyone else was trimming just the leaves that stuck out from the bud. So, he started nipping the little leaves off. Nip, snip, nip, all the way around the bud. It didn't seem as big when he finished and he wondered if he was doing it wrong, but everyone else's seemed about the same so he kept going. He picked up another and repeated the process.

Everyone was talking and laughing. Mia brought coffee. No one talked to Oliver. No one had said, "don't talk to Oliver," it just seemed like it was understood that he didn't want to talk. So no one did. Once, when Star who was sitting directly to Oliver's right got up, she steadied herself by putting her left hand on his shoulder, and as she did, she gave a double squeeze. Oliver looked up and caught a glimpse of something in her eyes. In her smile. For maybe the first time since this whole trip started, Oliver was thinking about something other than his problems.

"Hey fuckers, ya'll want to go on a field trip," said Jackson. "We're going to Moonstone Beach?"

϶ϵ

Moonstone beach was a few miles south along Highway 101. At Moonstone there were huge boulders protruding from the shore line and what seemed to be a river, coming in from somewhere. It was 4 o'clock in the afternoon and the sky was as blue as water.

Jackson and Chewy both grabbed big duffle bags from the back of Jackson's truck.

"This rock over here is the one we're going to climb," said Jackson, pointing to a large rock face overlooking the beach. "Anybody who wants to climb can go up."

Jackson and Chewy disappeared into what looked to be a tunnel of bushes along the side of the rock.

"Oliver," said Charlie. "Are you going to climb that?"

"Fuck no," said Oliver. "I like being down here."

"I want to climb it," said Megan.

"Oliver's not a big fan of heights," said Charlie. "When we were kids he didn't even like climbing up to the top of the monkey bars."

"Clear," they heard Jackson shout from the top, as two ropes came falling down and hung to the bottom of the rock.

"Clear," shouted Chewy, and two more ropes fell 100 feet to the right.

"It's not so bad," said Star, "we're top roping. That means that there is always a rope anchored to the top. You can't fall because the person on the bottom always has the rope ready to stop you."

Chewy and Jackson came around the corner of the rock. "Who's first," said Jackson.

"I'll go," said Star.

Mia and her friend Sam from Berkley approached the right side rope that looked harder than the one on the left.

"On belay," said Star.

"Belay on," said Jackson.

"Climbing," said Star, and she started up the rock.

"What are they saying?" asked Charlie.

"I don't know," said Oliver. "Something about belay or something."

"On belay," said Mia.

"Belay on," said Sam.

"Climbing," said Mia, and she started up the face of the rock.

"They are saying, 'on belay,' and 'belay on.' They are communicating to each other that they are ready to climb," said Chewy. "When you start climbing you want your partner on the ground to be ready and not looking off at a bird in the sky. It's just a reminder. Safety is always the first priority."

Star was almost half way up the rock face above them. Mia on the other side was almost at the top. She looked like a cat, thought Oliver. She balanced on one bent leg, reached across and grabbed a small crack and hooked her free toe on a little edge, with her free hand she reached as far up as she could and grabbed a little knob that was barely sticking out of the otherwise smooth rock face. She moved her hands again, then her feet, smooth and methodically. From the ground the final 30 feet looked completely smooth and she glided up as though she were dancing. When she reached the top, she let her hands go and fell back on the rope. Sam let out some slack and Mia bounded backwards down the rock to the bottom.

On the left side, Star also reached the top, and let her hands go, trusting the rope and her partner to lower her to the ground.

"Who's next?" said Jackson.

"I'll go," said Charlie.

"Put a harness on," said Jackson. "I'll give you a hand tying in when you have it on."

"How do you put this thing on?" said Charlie.

"Like this," said Megan. She helped him into the harness and tied his rope. "You make a figure 8 like this, then thread the rope back through like this."

Charlie looked up at the rock then walked up to it. He grabbed the rock and started to climb. About five feet up his left hand slipped. "Shit," he said, and kept climbing. He was doing good, slow, but steady. Sam and Chewy both climbed the harder route in the time it took Charlie to reach the top, but he made it. "Okay," he shouted. "I'm at the top."

"You have to let go," yelled Megan.

"How do I do that," Charlie yelled back.

"Let go with your hands," shouted Megan.

Charlie let go with one hand, then the other and was surprise to find that his whole weight was supported by the rope, like he was in a swing.

"Lean back," said Jackson, "and push off with your feet as you come down."

"Holy shit, I did it," said Charlie, when he got back on his feet on the ground.

"Your turn Oliver," said Jackson.

"No," said Oliver.

"Chewy, take over here," said Jackson. "Come over here Oliver, let's have a talk."

"I don't know what there is to talk about," said Oliver. "I don't want to climb that rock."

"Let's go for a little walk," said Jackson.

Jackson walked with Oliver over to a little pile of boulders and sat down.

"So what's the problem, Oliver."

"I don't like heights. I have no interest in climbing."

"What do you think will invoke more fear? Climbing a rock with a rope attached to you, where if you fall, chances are the worst that will happen, will be to get a few scratches, or driving across the country with a carload of weed where the consequences are going to prison for an extended period of time."

"I don't have anything to prove to you," said Oliver.

"Fuck if you don't," said Jackson. "You think I'm going to send you across this god forsaken country with all that shit if I don't trust you? If you can't handle yourself you might as well pack your shit and go."

"How is climbing that rock going to prove anything? Why do you even care so much? I'm scared of heights, don't you get it? There. Yeah, I'm scared. Who wouldn't be scared? I could lose everything. I've been working my whole life to be this, great kid. I was always the good one. I was always the one who had my shit in order. I washed my own clothes when I was 6. I started cleaning up after my mom and my brother when I was probably 7. I got straight A's because I wanted everyone to see what a good kid I was. I've spent my whole life proving shit. But I'm a chicken shit, okay. Is that what you needed to hear?"

"Fuck that kid. You got straight A's because you're smart. Because you did the work. You ever look in the mirror Oliver? You ever really look at yourself in the mirror and meet the real you? You need to look into your eyes and meet yourself. Get past all the bullshit. All that self-pity bullshit that's holding you in that cage of yours."

"Who the fuck are you to tell me shit. You think you're my dad? You think you're my big brother? Why the fuck do you care?"

"You see this hat I wear? This dude, the dude that owned this hat was a general in Napoleon's army. He fought and killed for a cause. He led men into battle. Men who didn't owe him shit either. He didn't owe them anything. Yet it was his duty to be there for them."

"That's a bunch of shit," said Oliver.

"Ha," said Jackson. "You're probably right. Nevertheless. Your brother is my brother, and I'm starting to like you."

"How does you liking me keep me from getting locked up on my way home from here?" said Oliver.

"You're the only one who can do that," said Jackson. "Just like you got all those A's in school. You need to keep your head in the game. You need to not let fear be your deciding factor. Fear is a natural thing. It is a good thing, to a point. You need to learn to listen to it, and then move through it. I'll make you a deal. I'm going to give you this hat. If you agree to wear this hat for the rest of the time you are here, you don't have to climb. You do have to wear this hat wherever you go. You have to accept the hat. It takes bravery to pull off a hat like this. What do you say? Are you in?"

"You're nuts," said Oliver.

"Without question," said Jackson.

"Who is my brother? I mean, who is this Big Roy guy and is he my brother?"

"When your brother got into this whole business he thought we should have code names. He wanted me to call him Big Roy, and if that's who he wanted to be that's who he was."

"Why did he lie to me all this time?"

"He's the only one who can tell you that," said Jackson.

"What was your code name?" said Oliver.

"Jackson. My dad was a dick. He always pushed us. Never told us we were doing good, just made us work harder. He was a football coach in a place where football was the center of the universe. He wanted a varsity quarterback for a son, so I became a quarterback. He wanted to take state, so I worked my ass off for him and we made it to state. During the state championship I rolled my ankle. I stuck it out, but I just couldn't get my leg to do what I needed it to do, no matter how much I pushed it. I got sacked 5 times in about 6 plays, but my dad wouldn't take me out of the game. I did so much for that man. I worked and pushed and killed myself a little every day for that man. I walked off the field. That was the last time I ever played football. The man hasn't talked to me since. All that shit I did. I thought for all those years that I did it for him. It wasn't until I looked inside into my true nature that I realized I did all for me. It was something I needed at the time. Jackson is my code name. I used to have a different name. I left that life behind a long time ago."

"I'll take it. I'll wear the hat," said Oliver. "I'm wearing it with the points front to back though."

"Your choice," said Jackson. "Just be careful with it. That hat cost more than your van."

Oliver put the hat on his head. It felt a little awkward. He tried it from side to side at first, and it seemed to fit okay, but when he put it front to back it felt almost right.

"Holy shit, captain," said Charlie, when they reached the rock again. "Nice hat."

"I kind of like it," said Star. "It makes you look distinguished."

"It feels kind of weird. Jackson said I have to wear it," said Oliver.

"You don't have to do anything you don't want to kid," said Jackson.

"I want to climb," said Oliver.

"Here you go," said Jackson. "Step into this harness."

Star helped him into his harness and tied him off. "Are you going to wear the hat?" she asked.

"I'm wearing it," smiled Oliver.

"Here's the thing," said Jackson. "People say, 'don't look down,' but that's bullshit. Look down as often as you like. If you feel like you're going to fall, look down. It'll help you hang on tighter."

"Climbing is really about being in the moment," said Mia, who had come over from the other route. "If you are concentrating on what you are doing you won't have much time to think about looking down. Climb with your feet. Use them to push you up as much as you can. Most people when starting out tend to pull themselves up with their arms."

"How do I know Jackson won't accidentally drop me when I fall," said Oliver.

"You don't," said Mia. "You're job when you climb is to think about what you're doing. His job is the think about what he's doing. That's what makes the partnership work. Your job is to keep in contact with the rock. His job is to anticipate if you are in danger, and always be ready to act. Your job is to concentrate."

"Okay," said Oliver. "I'm ready."

"Say on belay," whispered Star.

"On belay," said Oliver.

"Belay on," said Jackson.

"Say climbing," whispered Star.

"Climbing," said Oliver.

"Climb on," said Jackson.

Oliver took a deep breath and looked up. The rock seemed to tower straight up over his head. He leaned in and reached over his head to a large pocket in the rock. It felt cold and hard. The whole rock seemed to radiate cold in the warm late afternoon sun. He stepped up onto a little rock that jutted out from near the bottom, and began to climb. He noticed that the closer he got the more places he saw to grab and step. He was making his way up pretty smoothly, he thought.

Then he looked down. Holy shit. He was probably twenty feet off the ground, but it seemed a lot higher. How was he supposed to make it all the way to the top? His arms were already starting to hurt. He reached up and grabbed a rock and his hand popped off. He didn't fall, but it hurt like hell. He looked at his middle finger and it looked like the fingerprint had been scraped off by sand paper.

He kept going. He was starting to sweat and it dripped from his brow under the hat, which he had to keep pushing up. He thought he was about half way now. There was a little ledge here that he hadn't seen from the ground. He rested for a minute and looked around. The view was actually pretty amazing.

The further he climbed up, the easier it seemed to get. The handholds were bigger, and although his arms were getting tired, he tried to climb with his feet as much as he could.

And then. He was there. Shit. Now he had to get down. He looked around, and it looked much higher than it did from the bottom. The people on the ground didn't quite look like ants, but maybe the size of squirrels.

He grabbed the large ring bolted to the rock that the rope ran through just above him. It felt solid. He thought about climbing straight up from here and just untying the rope at the top. He could walk down the same way Jackson and Chewy walked down when they tied the ropes up here.

"Lean back," yelled Megan from the bottom. "Just let go and lean back against the rope."

He wanted to let go. He really did. He looked down. Oh shit. Jackson was right, looking down makes you want to hold on tighter.

"Just lean back," said Mia. "Focus on where you are in the moment. Focus on where your body is. Focus on where your feet are. Focus where your hands are. Don't worry about where you are relative to the ground. Think about where you are relative to the points of contact you have to the rock, and the rope."

The rope was tight. Oliver let one hand go, then the other. Amazing, it was like sitting in a swing. He slowly started to drop. Oh, no. And he stopped. That wasn't too bad. He looked at the rock where his feet were and he dropped again. This time he was ready. He caught himself, and pushed out just slightly, almost instinctively, and swung gently to the next spot and placed his feet. This wasn't that bad. A couple more gentle swings and he was resting on the bottom.

"Nice work," said Jackson. "You did good kid. You ready to go up again?"

"Yeah, it wasn't that bad," said Oliver. "Little too tired to go up again."

"What do you think," said Charlie. "Pretty cool right?"

"Different," said Oliver. "Good."

The sun was starting to go down over the water. Jackson lit a joint and they started packing the ropes and the gear.

"Isn't weed still illegal here?" said Oliver. "You can't smoke in a public place can you?"

"Look around," said Star. "What do you think those people are doing right there." She pointed to a circle of college age kids sitting on a rock near the shore. "No one will mess with us here."

"All right kids. Time to pack up," said Jackson. "We have work to do. We party at the end of the week. Now we go."

Oliver took a long drag as the joint was passed around, and started walking back to the car. He stopped and turned before the parking lot, taking it all in one last time. The boulders jutting from the sand at the edge of the beach. The pink purple orange sky streaked with white wisps of translucent clouds. He tasted the sea in the air, the life and death in it.

"Race you to the car," said Charlie, already passing him, kicking up sand in his wake.

And he was off. Following in the footsteps then passing them in the soft sand.

15

"Are we going with the girls in the morning?" asked Charlie.

"I don't know," said Oliver. "Seems like a long way out of our way."

"How do you mean?" said Charlie. "We're already here. Megan said it's only an hour away."

"We won't be back till Thursday," said Oliver.

"Oliver, who knows when Jackson is going to have our shit, we need to stop worrying about that. Besides, did you hear about that thing Friday night? I guess there is going to be some kind of big harvest party at this place called Horse Mountain. I think it's going to be worth sticking around for."

"Yeah, I heard. I think I'm the only one here who cares that I don't have all the time in the world. No one here operates on a normal time schedule, with responsibilities and reality to deal with."

"I'm having a great time here," said Charlie. "I think this Megan girl really likes me. I really like her. It's like she doesn't even see me like all the other girls back home. She thinks I'm cool. I kind of want to marry her."

"Shut up. You barely know each other. You've held her boob. That's it."

"She has really nice boobs."

"Don't be stupid."

"Why not? Why can't I be stupid? What if we need to be stupid sometimes to learn how to be not stupid," said Charlie.

"That doesn't even make sense," said Oliver.

"It totally makes sense. We can't go around thinking we are doing everything right all the time just because it's what we are supposed to do. The Wright brothers weren't supposed to fly. That was stupid. Christopher Columbus wasn't supposed to sail the ocean blue. He was supposed to fall off the earth. That was pretty stupid. We do what we are told all the time because it's supposed to be the right thing to do. Because it's supposed to be 'not stupid.' Look where it has got me so far. I live in an apartment by myself in a city that I've lived in all my life and still know almost no one. Everyone from high school has pretty much left. I don't have anything in common with the college kids there. I feel alone most of the time with people all around me. I think that's stupid. I work at a sandwich shop, with no prospects for advancement. I think that's stupid. What am I doing with my life Oliver? What else is there for me out there?"

"I'm sorry Charlie. I didn't mean to call you stupid."

"What the fuck are you going to do when we get back anyway? You have almost two weeks before school starts. I know your mom is sick, but she's not going to be any more or less sick with you sitting next to her. You would probably be at my house playing video games anyway. Please Oliver. I want to do this thing, whatever it is. Whatever we are doing out here I want to do it for a little bit longer."

"It's not going to last forever you know," said Oliver.

"Hey guys," said Megan, coming out through the back patio door.

"Are you to trying to hog all this fresh night air?" said Star.

"We're just..." said Oliver.

"We're going with you," said Charlie, breaking in. "When do we leave?"

"Right on," said Star. "I'll tell the parents to make some room. We'll go in the morning."

"Do you smell that," said Megan, reaching over and putting her hand on Charlie's leg. "Pine and ocean, the best two smells ever, all combined into one."

Star reached over and grabbed Oliver's hand. She led him to the back of the house, out of sight of the patio.

"I want to kiss you," she said.

"Why," said Oliver.

"Because you're cute and mysterious. I like you."

"I'm just not used to hot girls liking me," said Oliver.

"Do you always make it this hard to kiss you?" she laughed. "Maybe this is why you're not used to it. You don't know how to take a hint even when it's not just a hint."

She grabbed him around the waste and kissed him. Any resistance Oliver had melted away. He gave in. He embraced it. He felt her tongue probing his mouth and in turn took the time to explore hers.

With his hands he felt her face and moved them down to her long neck. His fingers pulsed with energy. Everything he touched was more sensitive than usual.

He could hear her breathing. Soft breaths as he moved his hands down to the smooth skin under her t-shirt. He ran his hand up her back on the inside of her shirt and kissed her hard.

"Let's go inside," she whispered.

She led him by the hand, past the patio where Charlie and Megan sat, into the kitchen and through the living room passed the other trimmers who were at the table laughing and working. Almost no one noticed.

Oliver had had sex before. He dated Becky in college for two years and 4 months. In that time they had sex exactly 6 times. The first two times she wanted it. She wanted to see what all the fuss was about. She didn't want Oliver to see her all the way naked. Not yet. She had to save something for marriage. There were rules. He could touch her boobs under her shirt, but he couldn't touch her butt or her stomach. They had to be under the covers and under no circumstance could he look at her vagina. She called it her va-jay-jay.

The first time lasted almost a minute. She was upset. She had really hoped her first time would be amazing.

She bought Oliver some books. She even helped him practice a couple of times with her hand. She read in a magazine that if he was feeling himself get really close to coming he was supposed to stop and refocus. "We have to communicate," she would say. Her idea was that if she stroked him to almost the point of coming then stop, he would learn to hold it.

The second time she let him see her boobs. It lasted a little less than a minute. He tried to slow down and stop, he just couldn't bring himself to do it, and it was over. He rolled over out of breath. She pushed the covers away and grabbed her clothes and left the room crying.

Over the course of the next two years they had sex exactly 4 more times. Once she tried to get him drunk, that didn't work. The last three he had to beg for. Each time involving what seemed like days of planning, gifts, favors, and in the end she was always disappointed. When they broke up, she told him she needed a real man. Someone who knew how to take control. He thought that was a little strange, since she so totally controlled every aspect of their relationship. He was left feeling defeated, and weak.

This felt different. Star didn't ask him to do anything. Nor did she make him ask permission. She gave and she took, but only in rhythm with what Oliver gave and took.

"I'm sorry," Oliver said when he finished.

"Shhh...sorry for what," she whispered.

"For finishing so soon."

"It doesn't have to be over."

"It doesn't," he said.

"We have more condoms."

For the next two hours they explored. Each of them exploring the other, with hands and tongues and smiles and breaths.

A hard knocking came on the door.

"Oliver," said Charlie in a whisper that sounded more like a yell. "Oliver."

Oliver laid back and put his hand on his head.

Star smiled, "you better answer that."

They both got out of bed and put their clothes back on.

"What the fuck is it Charlie?" Oliver said when they had reached the kitchen.

"Dude, I did it," said Charlie.

"You did what?" said Oliver.

"I got laid. Let's go outside, I don't want everyone to hear."

They stepped outside.

"We went down to the beach and brought a couple of blankets. We did it Oliver. I did it."

"I'm happy for you Charlie," said Oliver.

"What were you guys doing in there? Did you? You know? Did you guys do it too?"

"I don't really want to talk about it, Charlie."

"Quit being a dick. You got laid. I can see it in your face, fucker."

Oliver smiled, just a little bit.

16

The four of them, Oliver, Star, Charlie and Megan all woke up in the same bed again on Wednesday morning. Not that Oliver liked it a whole lot. In the middle of the night he had to kick Charlie and Megan down to the floor so he didn't have to try and sleep while they did it next to him. Eventually, at some point in the night they moved back up into the bed.

Charlie got out of bed when he smelled bacon and eggs, and Megan followed.

"I just need to tell you," said Star. "Don't be alarmed by the guns at my parents' house."

"What?" said Oliver.

"My dad has a lot of guns," said Star. "He's not a violent person, and he would never use them unless he was in danger. He will probably be carrying one on his belt."

"Holy shit. What if he finds out that we, you know?" said Oliver.

"That we what?" she smiled.

"That we, you know… made love," said Oliver.

"We made love," she laughed. "Oliver, do you love me? I don't even know your last name."

"You know what I mean," said Oliver.

"I'm just kidding," said Star. "He's cool though. He's an old school hippie. You know free love and all that stuff."

"I thought old hippies were like pacifists. Why does he have a bunch of guns?"

"He is kind of a pacifist, but it's complicated I guess. He's a realist too. He's got weed. Lots of it growing. People do come and try to steel it sometimes. He isn't just going to say go ahead you can take it. It's how he feeds his family and puts a roof over their heads. If someone came by one year and stole his crop, and he said, 'go ahead take it. You must need it more than me.' The next year they would just come back and do the same thing and he would be growing for them, for free at that point. The way things are you have to pretty much protect yourself. With medical marijuana, he is growing pretty much within his legal state rights. He is in a co-op and they grow for a lot of people with real medical needs, who can't or don't know how to grow their own crops. According to the state, everything they do is above board. Federal is a different story. The feds could come in and take everything down anytime, and send him to jail. That's not what the guns are for though. This time of year it's almost harvest. He has to watch his garden, because sometimes people, mostly kids, will come in and try to make off with some plants. I don't think he could actually shoot anybody, but he has had to fire warning shots."

"That sounds really intense. It sounds stressful," said Oliver.

"You know, my dad's a really laid back guy most of the time. He surfs and that keeps him calm. This time of the year is the most stressful, but it's cool. I don't want to scare you off. I just wanted to tell you what we are going into."

"Are you sure they want us there?" said Oliver.

"Of course. They love meeting my friends. They're good people. They really are. Probably a little different than your family, but different is good right?"

"Different is pretty good most of the time," said Oliver. "This whole trip has been totally different to me. I'm still getting used to this place. By the way, my last name is Worth."

"Oliver Worth. I like that. Let's get up and get some of those eggs," said Star. "They have some of the best eggs I've ever had. My last name is Peoples. Don't even laugh, I know, Star Lover Peoples. I still have no idea what my parents were thinking naming me Star Peoples. I guess my last name is Scottish or something."

"No way? Your middle name is Lover?"

"That's what my birth certificate says," said Star.

They got up and walked to the kitchen. The rest of the trimmers were already up and either eating breakfast or off on some sort of morning adventure. Jackson and Chewy were in the kitchen sharing a joint.

"Good morning kids," said Jackson. "Easy over or sunny side up?"

"Can you do scrambled?" said Oliver.

"A scrambled egg is a broken dream, my friend," said Jackson. "For you Oliver, I will kill your dream. Nice hat, by the way."

"Thanks, I'm getting used to it."

"How do you think Star's parents are going to like it," said Jackson.

"I think they will love it," said Star.

"Shit, I didn't even think about that. Are they going to think I'm an idiot?" said Oliver.

"No," said Star. "I think they will like you more for it," she smiled. "Just don't tell them the thing about it costing $18,000. They might think you're some kind of nut job for wearing that thing around."

"Tell them you're a pirate," said Jackson. "A writer pirate, coming to take their daughter off to the edges of the earth in search of booty."

"It gives you character," said Chewy.

"I feel like a character," said Oliver, "in some crazy story where I'm the star and locked into a dream that I can't wake up from."

"Is it a good dream?" said Star.

"Yeah, it's seems like it's getting better," said Oliver.

"You are not the only one my friend," said Jackson. "Millions of people are sleep walking all over this crazy world every day. They get up and look in the mirror and think...as little as possible. I didn't make that up I heard it somewhere, but you get my point? It's like we evolved for hundreds of thousands of years as these animals that used our intelligence to survive. Every day was a struggle. Every day was a fight for survival. Now in our society so many people live these completely sedentary lives. They wake up in the morning and everything is taken care of for them. They brush their teeth, drive to work, do their job, come home, watch TV, rinse and repeat. They are taken care of as if they are still in their mothers shadow from birth to death. Never having to venture out into the harsh reality of the world. They are told do this, and they do, do that, and they do. They feel like they are making the right decision because everything goes smoothly. They crave that smooth trajectory. God forbid something happens to shake things up a little. Losing a job is like the end of the world as they know it. The only thing they can do is get a new one as fast as they can, so they can get back safe into their little comfortable cocoon, curl up into a ball and watch TV in comfort at the end of the night. Trying desperately to get back to a place where they no longer have to make hard decisions, or think too much. Sorry, I forgot, did you guys want bacon?"

"Yes, please," said Oliver.

"That's one reason I like you. You're polite. I'm serious. It's a dying art. Do you know what the word Apocalypse means, Oliver," said Jackson, pointing at Oliver with the spatula.

"Isn't it like the end of the world or something? From the bible?" said Oliver.

"It means, lifting of the veil," said Jackson. "The thing is, everybody thinks we all have it figured out. Every generation of Western Europeans for the last couple of thousand years, has thought we knew pretty much everything there is to know, except for a couple of things. They have all thought that since they were on the cutting edge of technology they were just about to have it all figured out.

Back when that hat was made in the late 1700s, they had gun powder. They had cannons. They had mastered the art of taking rocks out of the ground and turning them into metal that they could use to make weapons and forks and door handles. The world was no longer flat. Go back to the age of Jesus Christ and go to Jerusalem. They had it all figured out. The priests made sacrifices to God at the temple and as long as they could afford to give an animal to the priest to have slaughtered, they were doing well in the eyes of the Lord. Yes they were being held captive by the Romans, but that was pretty easily explained too. Ask Jesus. At this point most of the pyramids, and certainly the Sphinx had already been constructed with the latest technologies of the day.

If you would have told the priests of Christopher Columbus's day, that in a few hundred years you could get into a long metal tube with wings and fly across the ocean in an afternoon, they would probably have tied you to a stake and burned those ideas right out of the world."

"I'm not sure I follow?" said Oliver.

"The priests of the day told the people they had it all figured out. They had the real truth. That they had power over the real truth and all you had to do was believe them. That there was nothing left to figure out, because God had told a chosen few saints all the answers and they were all written down in a divine book. The people only had to listen to the priest and believe every word he said, to know the truth about everything. In this way we were trained not to think. We have, for generation upon generation, been taught that we have it all just about figured out. And now we have science, which in my humble opinion is on the right track, but tends to get institutionalized and caught up in dogma, and can end up being a sad excuse for an atheistic religion," said Jackson. "We think our history, the stories we are told of the heroes of our past, and the science, and our medicine have almost all the answers figure. We travel through this world comfortable in that knowledge. It's all like one big dream state that is drifted on through."

"Maybe," said Chewy, smiling. "You feel like you're in a dream, because you're on the edge of waking up?"

"Jackson, you sound more and more like my dad, every time I come down here," laughed Star. "Let's eat, Oliver. You and your hat are coming with me."

"If you want to wake up, Oliver," said Jackson. "You have to be history. You have to push your head out of the membrane of your cocoon, and be the hero that the stories are told about. You have to take the journey and find out that the unknown is a real thing. You have to figure out some kind of answer and bring it back for the rest of us. You have to lift your vail and see the world as it really is."

"Why me? Why are you telling me all this stuff?" said Oliver.

"You are the one who said it felt like you are dreaming, I was telling you that you are right," laughed Jackson.

"I was joking," said Oliver.

"Just because you don't think you asked a question, doesn't mean you didn't," said Jackson. "If it means something to you, you'll know. If not, it doesn't much matter."

"All right boys," said Star. "We need to get going soon."

"What is the truth then?" asked Oliver. "What is the answer? What do I have to learn?"

"You will know," said Jackson, "when you wake up."

16.5

It was a warm sunny morning as they drove south down Highway 101. It was the first time Oliver and Charlie had seen the large redwoods in the day light. The massive trees towered over the ground and some seemed to be hundreds of feet high.

"I've never seen the redwoods before," said Oliver.

"Some trees in this area were here over 2000 years ago when Jesus was alive, or at least when our calendar begins," said Star. "A lot of the trees have been aged, and the forest service knows which trees are the oldest and the tallest, but won't tell the general public because some asshole might come out and try and cut the oldest or tallest tree alive down, just to say he did it."

They drove down the Redwood Highway section of the 101 and got off in Redway. The two way highway they were on now was much curvier than the 101 and the trees were much closer to the road in spots. If a person was claustrophobic they may have been uncomfortable. They dove down the paved road for about 25 minutes, then turned off on a gravel road and then to dirt. Charlie and Megan were in the back seat attached at the lips.

"How far out do your parents live," asked Oliver.

"They live pretty far in the sticks," said Star. "My dad always said his goal was to live closer to the ocean than to the nearest town. They live about ten minutes from the beach, and fifteen from the nearest town, which isn't really that much of a town. I always thought it was cool growing up in the woods, and on the beach. We surfed every chance we got. If there was a nice swell coming in, we were out there at dawn, and if it was a really nice break, even school could wait till we had our fill. My dad has never been one for being on time and he never really pushed us in that direction, except when it was time to surf."

"Did you guys ever get lonely out here, there doesn't seem to be a lot of people around," said Oliver.

"My sister and I had a lot of adventures in these woods and played a lot of fun games that we made up. We would tell each other stories and pretend we had met the Fairies. When I was real young, I was convinced that I actually had.

For the most part, it wasn't that lonely. My parents had friends over playing music or just talking around the camp fire, what seemed to me at the time like almost every night. It was at least a couple of times a week that we had friends over. Lots of them had kids our age, and all the kids around here knew each other. Everyone in our scene hung out at the Mateal Community Center and all of us kids played together while the grownups talked about grown up things."

The driveway to the house was a long dirt road, bumpy from water washed ruts in places. Out of the narrow pathway a little clearing appeared in front of them and a really nice looking cabin. At the end of the driveway, nearest to the house, stood a man wearing a cowboy hat. He carried a rifle and clearly had a pistol in a holster on his hip.

Charlie and Megan unlocked long enough to see the man standing there.

"Holy shit," said Charlie. "That dude has a gun. Where the fuck are we?"

"Relax," said Star. "That's my dad."

"Is he planning on killing us?"

"No Charlie, you're just fine," said Star, "unless he catches you making out with Megan. He's killed people for a lot less."

"What the fuck," said Charlie. "Oliver, what are you getting us into here?"

"Relax, Charlie," said Star. "I'm messing with you. My dad wouldn't hurt a fly."

"With those guns, he could hurt more than a fly if he wanted to."

"Hey kids," said Star's dad. "Have you guys eaten, Star's mom is just about to make some lunch." He wrapped Star up in a big bear hug. "Hello Megan, how are you."

"I'm good Bill," said Megan. "How are you?"

"Couldn't be better."

"Are you a real cowboy?" said Charlie.

"Ha, I'm about as real of a cowboy as your friend here is a pirate. I'm Bill," he said reaching his hand out to shake Charlie's, and then Oliver's. "My friends call me 'Wild Bill' you can call me Bill, or William or whatever you want really. You can call me a cowboy if you want, I've been called a lot worse," he smiled.

Bill, whose friends called Wild Bill, but his real name was William, showed them into the house. The inside of the cabin was beautiful. Large picture windows let in an amazing amount of light for how dark it was in some parts of the woods around the house. The walls were covered in clear stained boards and you could see all the knots and imperfections. It didn't look like any of the boards were cut in straight vertical lines as, say, a 2x4 with one straight edge running the full length. The walls looked as though the boards had been cut from the tree in slices and put straight on the wall. Some were four inches tall some were twelve inches tall, all pieced together and fit with what seemed like amazing precision.

"My dad made this place," said Star. "When did you build it, Dad? Back in the mid 90's?"

"Well I started in 1993. We were still doing quite a bit of traveling then. We lived in a Winnebago for the first year we were out here, while I scraped the money together to buy nails and do what I could to get the materials I needed from the local saw mill. We were living in her by the end of 1994."

"This is my Mom, Melissa," said Star. "Most people call her Mel."

"It's mom to you," she winked at Star, giving her a big hug.

"And this is my sister, Taylor," she said.

"Hey everybody," said Taylor. She was a tall, skinny, smiley blond girl, 17 and going into her senior year of high school in a couple of weeks. "Hate to hug and run," she said to Star, "but I'm off. I got plans with some friends this afternoon. We're going diving for abalone at a spot around Shelter Cove. Are you going to surf with us in the morning?"

"I wouldn't miss it sis. Love you," said Star, as Taylor grabbed a pair of goggles and swim fins off the counter and headed out the door.

"Hope you kids are hungry," said Mel. "I made a big pot of vegetarian chili. I wasn't sure how big of an appetite these boys you were bringing would have, so I made plenty."

Mel was standing behind the stove, which was centered in the middle of a large island that separated the kitchen from the living room in the large open space. There were stools at the front of the island and Bill sat down and took off his hat.

"This is a really nice place you have here," said Oliver. "It doesn't look this big from the outside."

"We like it," said Bill. "Always something to be done. It's kind of been like one big art project."

"Do you guys smoke," said Bill, pulling a joint from the band of his hat.

"Yes, please," said Charlie.

"Sometimes...I mean, lately I have been. I mean yes, I guess," said Oliver, not sure exactly what to say. He wasn't used to the idea of an adult pulling out a joint to smoke. At least not a parent. Even if he knew that they grew pot, which was new to him too.

"Sit, please," said Bill, lighting the joint. "Make yourself at home. Our house is your house."

Everyone sat down on the stools around the island, and Mel ladled out large bowls of amazing smelling chili.

"What brings you boys to town?" asked Bill.

"Well, sir," said Oliver. "We are. Well."

"It's okay," said Star. "You can be honest here. They're picking up a load from Jackson."

A sudden sense of fear swept over Oliver. He had never really heard it said out loud. He had never heard it said to anyone he didn't know.

"I see," said Bill, taking a long thoughtful toke. "Where are you coming from, and going to?"

"We're from Wisconsin," said Charlie.

"That's a long ways," said Bill.

"It took us about two days to get here," said Charlie.

"Have you ever done anything like this before?" said Bill.

"No," said Oliver.

"Are you working for yourself?" said Bill. "Why did you come all this way?"

"My brother," said Oliver.

"He couldn't do it himself?" said Bill.

"He had other things going on I guess," said Oliver, now starting to get annoyed with the questions. He was starting to feel like a child being scolded.

"It's a shame that you boys have to drive all the way across the country for something that would grow just as well where you live," said Mel.

"There's a war going on over this stuff you know," said Bill. "This war on drugs. I think a change is in the air finally though. They legalized it in California, for medical use, quite a few years ago now. Medical...funny thing, medical marijuana. Yes, it helps many things. The people who need its cure the most are the ones who think it's the devils weed."

"Why is medical marijuana funny?" said Oliver. "Isn't it a good thing?"

"Good yes," said Bill. "As soon as it was legalized for medical use, two thirds of the people in northern California suddenly came down with some sort of chronic pain. Everybody went to the doctor and got a card. I was pretty suspect at first. I didn't want the government to have me on their records as being a pot smoker, but after a while I signed on too. You see I get these terrible neck aches. The only thing that cures it is this here weed. Well, that's my line to the doctor, who winks and hands me a prescription. I filled out the paper work and I am a legal pot smoker."

"Sounds pretty sweet to me," said Charlie. "I wish we could do that in Wisconsin."

"It's not a long term solution," said Bill. "Some of my fellow growers in the area, members of my co-op, like the situation just fine and would actually prefer it to stay illegal, but I, for one, am ready to just legalize it and be done with it all ready."

"Why would anyone who grows not want it legal?" said Oliver.

"Now you did it," smiled Star.

"Here's why," said Bill "and this comes in a couple of layers. First things first. It is legal here for medical use, and at the same time it isn't. It is legal with the state. You can be completely legitimate with the state and if you get too big, if you stick your head up out of the sand, the feds can come in and take your head off. It is not legal federally. If you have your card, you are allowed to grow a certain amount of plants, by state law. If you can't or don't know how to grow it, you can let someone else grow it for you. That is what my co-op does. We are totally above the boards with the state. We provide state approved legal marijuana to dispensaries around the area. If that dispensary gets too big, if one person grows a large amount of weed, again even legal with the state, the feds will come in and tear it all down and often lock you up to further make their point and set an example."

"So I don't get it, why wouldn't a grower want it legalized then?" said Oliver.

"The current state of the situation demands higher prices in the market," said Bill. "If it were legal, the fear is that the price would drop. Kids like you wouldn't risk their lives to drive all the way across the country to buy from us. You would just grow it in your own back yard. Or your closet. Or, in a perfect world, on your front lawn. Then there is big business. The little growers are scared that if companies like Philip Morris start growing and selling it the little guys won't be able to survive."

"I guess I see your point," said Oliver.

"Thing is... I think the fear is unfounded. Especially for guys like me. Pretty much everything I grow now is for local consumption anyway, that demand probably won't change much. My kids are almost out of the house, we don't have too many expenses here, and there isn't much we can't trade for besides gas for the truck."

The dogs started barking outside. Bill ran and grabbed his gun at the front door, and without saying a word, ran outside to check it out.

"I'm getting so tired of this," said Mel. "We're getting to old for this."

"Why do you still do it Mom?" said Star.

"We've done it so long now, it's who we are," said Mel. "We're just farmers. You know that dear. Your father is a man of principal, if he thinks something is worth doing, he likes to do it his way."

"If it's legal, even only with the state, can't the state cops help protect you?" said Oliver.

"Well this time of year they are pretty busy," said Mel. "There aren't that many cops in this area. The other fear is that they work with the feds if anything gets out of hand. The idea is not to raise any red flags. If you become noticed, it is generally a bad thing."

Bill, walked back into the house and the screen door cracked shut behind him as he leaned the gun against the corner by the entry way.

"Just the neighbor's dog snooping around," said Bill, sitting back down in his stool at the end of the island with his bowl of chili. "Why do you think marijuana is illegal, Oliver?"

"Well, it's against the law because it's a drug," said Oliver.

"Alcohol is a drug, caffeine is a drug, sugar is a powerful drug," said Bill.

"I think it's because it makes you high," said Charlie.

"What do you think Megan?" said Bill. "You've been pretty quiet over there this whole time."

"I think it's because people who are afraid of drugs, are afraid of weed, and they are afraid their kids will smoke it," said Megan.

"Don't they smoke it if they want to anyway?" said Bill. "When I was a kid, it was the kids who had all the weed. If I didn't live where I do, or grow it myself, I wouldn't know where to find it. I'm not a kid anymore. I'm an adult and I think I have the right to put anything in my body, or in my mind, that I like. Especially, marijuana. Have you ever heard of anyone dying from marijuana? Me either, and I've been around longer than you kids.

"I think it's like anything else. Use it with balance and use it with moderation and it really is a good medicine. I think that this message that we send to young people that drugs are bad, end of story, in the end is really doing a disservice. It's like telling kids just say no to sex. We have sex education classes to teach kids how to do it carefully because, they are kids and they experiment. I think it's much better to teach kids to be responsible. Don't do drugs unless you know the risks. Don't smoke a bunch of weed for the first time if you have to drive home in a half an hour, the same as with alcohol. I'm not against alcohol. I am for the responsible use of it. Don't take what Terence McKenna called a heroic dose of mushrooms unless you know what you are doing, otherwise you have a very likely chance of being in a world of hurt for quite a few hours, and possibly longer."

"Who is Terence McKenna," said Oliver. "I think I've heard of him before, but not sure where."

"He is a madman," said Mel. "When we lived down in Big Sur he used to come to our house, smoke all our weed and talk all night long. Bill would stay up all night listening to him and feeding him weed, until all the weed was gone and the sun was coming up. Then he would leave and Bill would be spouting crazy ideas for weeks."

"He was a brilliant man, Melissa," said Bill. "Eccentric, yes. He was a gifted raconteur and could wrap you up in a story and hold you there, almost hypnotized for hours."

"He thought the world was going to end on, what November 21, 2012?" said Mel. "Yet here we are. Several years later."

"He did have some crazy theories around the event horizon and the end of the world. I didn't really follow when he got on those tangents, although he was a very theory driven and science minded man. I heard him say on more than one occasion, that if the time got closer and it didn't look like it was going to happen, he would be willing to change his theory."

"Sounds like a hollow prediction to me," said Mel. "We shouldn't be turning the kids on to that craziness, Bill. We have to draw the line somewhere," she smiled.

"Terence had no lines, dear. There was no where he wouldn't explore. My point is still that education and knowledge is better than trying to pretend like it doesn't exist. Teach them about set and setting. Teach them not to do things they don't understand without the proper knowledge. Things like marijuana and even mushrooms are powerful tools of healing, if used in the right context. Either way, they are out there, they are naturally occurring substances that we can get directly from the earth and use without alteration or change to their structure at all. Almost as if they were meant for it.

"I don't think that drugs are bad for everyone, and also, I don't think that things like weed and mushrooms are good for everyone. Not everyone knows, for example, that if you are on an antidepressant or any form of SSRI, you should absolutely not take any form of hallucinogen, like mushrooms.

"Some people have adverse effects to many different things. I would argue that if a plant medicine shows you something, it is probably something that you need to look at and analyze. It's probably something you need to work on in your life. But use them with respect, and reverence."

"Okay, kids," said Mel. "I think we've had enough of a lesson for this afternoon. Who wants to go outside and get some fresh air?"

17

The dry air outside was thick with the smell of pine forest, and if the wind blew just right you could catch a hint of marijuana. The yard was very neat and tidy, except for the dozen or so chickens that ran around the yard pecking and scratching at the dirt. They had two dogs, Lucky and Merry Gold, who both looked like some kind of shaggy mix of mutt. In the middle of the yard was a large garden. Half of which had food such as tomatoes, broccoli, lettuce, etc. The other half was brimming with another plant.

They looked like marijuana bushes. They were at least 6 feet tall and each one so big around that Oliver wasn't sure two large men could reach each other if they put their arms around them. The girls walked up to the garden and started discussing how good the crop looked this year.

"Did you see Star's little sister?" said Charlie. "She was hot."

"Don't even go there, Charlie," said Oliver, as the two walked towards a bench that sat in the shade of the forest at the edge of the yard.

"I'm just saying, she's hot."

"Yeah, she is hot," conceded Oliver.

"What do you think of Megan?" said Charlie. "I really like her. She's like a wild animal. We had sex again this morning. In the shower. It's like she wants to do it all the time. It's amazing. It's the best thing ever, Oliver. I don't know if I'm going to be able to go back. What should I do?"

"What do you mean what should you do? Are you actually considering not going back? Like for real?" said Oliver.

"Kind of. What do I have back there besides an empty apartment? I see my parents once a year, at Christmas, when I get them presents. Other than that, it's mostly just you and you're going to college in a week. There are a couple other kids I could hang out with, but no one I really even like. Why not stay?" said Charlie.

"For one, you don't know anyone here. You don't have a job. You don't have a place to stay. Who's going to be there for you if things go wrong? Megan? You barely know her. She barely knows you. What are you going to do for food?" said Oliver.

"You sound exactly like your mom right now," said Charlie.

"Shit, you're right," said Oliver. "Come on though, Charlie. We've been out here for a few days. Do you really know what it's like out here?"

"How am I going to grow up if I never move out of my comfort zone? You have school. You already made it out of La Crosse. What about me? What do I have? I'll tell you. I don't have shit. I don't have an education. I don't have a career. I don't have a girlfriend. I have a job, maybe, when I get back, at a sandwich shop. As far as I know I only get one shot at this life thing, Oliver. What the fuck am I doing with it, besides sitting around on my ass all day wishing I was someone else? The thing is I'm never going to be someone else. I'm always going to be me. I am Charlie, this is who I am. I don't even know what that means. All I know is that I'm not getting anywhere doing the same thing I've been doing the three years since we've been out of high school."

"I just worry about you, is all," said Oliver. "You're like the only brother I ever really wanted. Don't get me wrong, I love Jeb. He's just so much different than me. I don't even understand how he can be so, I don't know, cool, and I'm not? He's always been the popular kid and he's never had to work hard for it. He was good in sports. Whatever, I don't hate Jeb. He's my brother and I love him, but you're like my brother who was always there for me."

"You can be a selfish asshole you know that. You see people for what they do for you. Not what they are for them," said Charlie, getting up off the bench and walking over to join everyone else, who at this point were laughing and apparently being entertained by a story from Bill near the garden.

Oliver sat alone on the bench. He was in a clearing surrounded by tall trees that seemed to be closing in all around him. He looked up and the blue sky was streaked with white clouds that seemed to be moving by faster than was even possible, as if the world were spinning faster than it should. He sat there and stared into space, watching the clouds speed by, until he thought he might be getting motion sickness. He closed his eyes, still staring off into space and the feeling of spinning only intensified. When he opened his eyes, Star was sitting next to him on the bench.

"Hello Oliver," she said.

"Hey Star," he said.

"Why are you sitting by yourself?" asked Star.

"Star, why do you think we're here?"

"Well, I brought you here," she said.

"No, I mean here on earth. What does all this mean?" he said.

"I don't know, Oliver."

"Sorry, I shouldn't be...you know, burdening you. I really like you Star. I'm trying really hard not to get all caught up in my head. It's kind of hard right now."

"I really like you too Oliver. It's not always easy for me to understand either. I don't think I know any more than you do."

"It just seems like we are all in this race and as you get older it gets faster and faster. We are in this race, but where does it go? Where is the end? I know we die and that's an end, but where do we go? What's the point of it all?" said Oliver.

"I don't know if there is a point to it all," said Star. "I think we are all like flowers in a garden. When the sun comes out we stand at attention and look at it. We are born in the spring and when the winter starts to come we wither and die. I don't know if flowers need a reason to live."

Oliver smiled. "You're pretty smart, Star," said Oliver. "How do you think I should tell that to my mom?"

"Tell her that she's a beautiful flower, and that you love her just the way she is," said Star.

"If I told her that, she would really think I'm on drugs," said Oliver.

"When we get back to Jackson and Mia's house, you should talk to Mia. She is like an angel in some ways, or like a shaman, I don't really know, but it's creepy sometimes the things she seems to know. From what I understand, she spent a year down in Peru, supposedly doing graduate work down there. She studied plant medicine and shamanism and spent a lot of time drinking Ayahuasca."

"What is Ayahuasca?" said Oliver.

"I guess they call it the Spirit Root. It's this root and leaf mixture that's boiled up by a Shaman into a tea. You drink the stuff and it's supposed to put you in touch with the spirit realm."

"That sounds pretty interesting," said Oliver.

"Sounds really scary to me," said Star. "I first met Jackson, and Chewy and your brother when she was down in the Amazon."

"You know my brother?" said Oliver.

"I met him when they were all in Oregon, working on Mt. Hood," said Star.

"How did you meet them? That was like four or five years ago. You were only a teenager then," said Oliver.

"I was 17. My parents let me go to this snowboarding school called Windells Snowboard Camp. It was my senior year of high school. It's this place that you can go to school, but also learn to become a pro snowboarder or skateboarder. It's a really cool place. We spent a lot of time on the mountain, and your brother and Chewy and Jackson worked on the ski hill at Timberline Lodge. It's the place where us kids from Windells took our snowboarding classes. I kind of had a thing for Chewy."

"What do you mean you kind of had a thing for Chewy?" said Oliver.

"You know, like a kid crush type thing. My girlfriends and I would always try to talk to them, and hang out with them. I got his phone number, and we would invite them to parties that we were going to. Chewy was like our age now at the time, like 22 or something. He pretty much ignored any sexual vibes I tried to put his way. He was a really good guy. I have to confess one thing though."

"Did you sleep with him?" Oliver said.

"No, I just told you he barely looked at me, and not in that way. I kind of kissed your brother," said Star.

"You kind of kissed him?" said Oliver.

"Kind of made out with him at a party," said Star.

"How old was my brother then, like 22 or 23. What a dick face. What in the hell was he doing messing around with a 17 year old?"

"It was kind of my fault. I came on to him pretty strong. I pretty much threw myself at him, as much as I knew how to do back then. I didn't really like him. Not much anyway. I was a stupid kid, trying to get Chewy's attention. I was trying to make him jealous."

"Did it work?" said Oliver.

"No, not at all. He barely noticed and it only made it worse," said Star.

"Is that what this is?" said Oliver. "Are you only with me to try and make Chewy jealous?"

"No, Oliver. That was a long time ago. After that year I kept in touch with him and Jackson. I went to college in Bend Oregon, and that's where I met Megan. For the past few years, since Jackson and Chewy moved to Northern Cali I've been coming down to trim a couple of times a year. It's fun, I make some cash, I get to see my folks."

"Have you done anything with Chewy since then?" said Oliver.

"No, Oliver. The first couple of times I came down I kind of hoped something would happen. I'm pretty sure Chewy has had a few girlfriends over the years, but he's kind of different. Who knows? I like him. He's a great friend, but there is no love connection," said Star.

"I can't believe you made out with my brother?" laughed Oliver.

"Shut up," said Star, smiling now. "I was a kid. I didn't know any better."

"I don't think I ever asked you? What are you going to school for?" said Oliver.

"I'm going for a double major in Biology and Natural Resource Management," said Star. "I'm going into my senior year. Megan is too. What about you, you're in a pretty big hurry to get back to school. You said you're an English major right? Why English?"

"I like to write," said Oliver. "It's kind of easy for me. It's a good way for me to deal with my issues and life in general. I can kind of figure things out by putting them on the page and reading them back to myself. It's kind of a weird way of looking into a mirror."

"That's really cool. You should write a story about this trip someday," said Star, reaching over and gently grabbing Oliver's hand.

"I don't think my mom would appreciate that very much," said Oliver.

"Hey let's go see what everyone else is up to," said Star. "It seems like we've been sitting over here forever." "Hold on a minute. My mom's calling. I'll be right there."

18

∞

"Hello Mom," said Oliver.

"Oliver, how is your trip? Are you in the forest? It sounds like you're in the forest?"

"Sort of. It's going well Mom. Charlie is having a great time."

"Have you heard from your brother? I can't get a hold of him. I've been calling his phone all day. He won't answer. I'm worried about him."

"Don't worry too much Mom. You know Jeb. He probably forgot to turn his phone on or something."

"Well I worry about you boys, that's my job. What will you two do when I'm gone?"

"I don't know Mom, probably live in peace."

"Oliver, you know better than talk to your mother like that. I am dying you know."

"Shit, I'm sorry Mom. I didn't mean it. I'm just frustrated I guess."

"What in the world do you have to be frustrated about? You. You are a young healthy boy. Your whole life is ahead of you. You are on a vacation by the ocean, doing god knows what with god knows who. If you aren't having the time of your life, it's your own fault."

"What is that supposed to mean Mom?"

"Are you going to tell me what's wrong, Oliver? Or are you going to make me guess? Fine I will guess. Oliver, you need to loosen up. Ever since you were a little boy you were too serious. There was always something bothering you. Something the world was doing that you just couldn't let go, or something you had to do that you couldn't stop thinking about. Ever since you were a little boy, you have been this way. Who am I to change that, I'm just your mom. As long as you're on this crazy holiday, you need to have fun with it. Have you even swam in the ocean yet? Did you know I almost swam in the ocean once? Your father and I went to the ocean once, in Florida. I was too scared to go in. I've always regretted that. I never got to taste the ocean. That sounds silly right? I wanted to taste it, I did. Oliver, you need to go in that ocean. You need to live your life. I can't do that for you."

"It's not that simple Mom. I wish it was."

"It's exactly that simple. You just need to let go, Oliver."

"How are you feeling Mom?"

"Don't worry about me? I will be just fine. Did you give any thought to my question?"

"What question?"

"Did you give any thought to my question about life, Oliver? What we are all here for? I'm nearing the end of my life. You have so much more to come. It's important for you to know what you are here for. I wouldn't have known to ask that if I wasn't where I am now. No one asked me that. I wish they would have."

"Don't talk like that Mom. You have a lot of life left. You can get through this. A lot of people beat cancer. You don't have to die."

"I'm not talking about me, Oliver. I'm talking about you. You need to live. Live with some sort of purpose. I had you boys. You were my purpose. You are why I am here. You don't need me anymore. You are a man now."

"I don't feel like a man, Mom. I don't feel any different than I did before. Why do you keep talking like this? It's like you're just giving up? Like you're just going to give in and let go."

"When I was a little girl, I wanted to be an astronaut. I read about the stars, I read anything I could get my hands on about space. My father got me a telescope for my 12th birthday. You know why I didn't try harder to become an astronaut, Oliver? Because I was scared. I was scared I couldn't do it. I was scared I wasn't smart enough. I was scared I wouldn't be brave enough. I never even tried. Maybe I wouldn't have been able to be an astronaut, but I didn't even go to college. I didn't go, because I was scared to fail.

I got to your age and thought to myself... 'I could be graduating college right now,' but I didn't go because I wasn't good enough. I was wrong Oliver. I was wrong to be so hard on myself. The difference between confidence and self-doubt is not very far apart. The difference is a choice. I see that now. The easy choice is to doubt yourself. You will always have that little voice in your head telling you that you can't, because you are not good enough. You need to ignore that voice. I am so thankful for you boys. I am thankful that I have had this wonderful life. The things I would do differently if I could, would be the things I didn't do because I was afraid."

"I'm afraid Mom. I'm so afraid of this. I don't feel like a man. I feel the same as I always have. I am scared for you. I don't want to lose you."

"Oliver, what I have is terminal. I am going to die. I am coming to terms with that. My mother has died. My father has died. Just like their mothers and fathers have all died. You will die someday too, Oliver. The question for you is not how you will die. The question is how you will live, in the face of it."

"Does it matter what I do? What's the point if I'm going to die anyway?"

"It matters more than you realize now, Oliver. It's hard for you, where you're at, to know what I have known from where I'm at. It's hard to communicate that with words. Just know that you need to live. You need to live with bravery and self-respect. That's all I ask of you."

"I will try Mom. I love you."

"I love you too, Oliver. Get home soon. I need to go now. It's Wednesday night, I have bingo. You be safe, Oliver. Tell Charlie I said hi."

"Okay Mom, bye."

∞

The sun, that had been high overhead most of the day made it's descent over the tops of the trees. It wasn't dark yet, but the light was casting long shadows over the yard with the promise of spinning into darkness.

Oliver sat on the bench at the edge of the yard with his phone in his hand. He laid down on the bench and fell asleep.

In his dream Oliver saw red and blue flashing lights. "Where did you get this?" They shouted. "Who sent you?" They shouted. They pulled a gun and shot. Oliver fell. It couldn't be. Everything started to slowly sink and spin at the same time. You can't die in your dreams. Is this what it felt like to die? He thought of his mom, she hugged him. He could see Jeb by his gravestone asking, begging, for forgiveness. He saw Mia. Mia, sitting in a yoga pose, saying something he didn't understand, there was light all around her. Was this the end? Was he really dying? Charlie was talking to him. Was Charlie an angel? His voice was getting louder and louder.

"Oliver... Oliver, wake up man," said Charlie.

"What, what's going on? How long was I asleep?"

"How would I know, I've been looking all over for you though. Why are you sleeping on this bench?"

"I was talking to my mom on the phone... and I must have passed out here."

"Oliver, we did it again. There was this tree house in the woods, she took me to it. This chick is crazy. I think I love her."

"You're being crazy Charlie," Oliver scratched his head. "You barely know her. Do you even know her last name?"

"It's Olson. Megan Olson. She's from Green Bay. Her parents have a little cabin on the lake in Northern Wisconsin. She was just home for a month and got back to Oregon just in time for her and Star to come down to Jackson's house. She is a Recreation Management major in college. She wants to be a physical education teacher. I told her she is really good at her job already. And she thought it was funny. She thinks I'm funny, Oliver. How crazy is that?"

"Super crazy," said Oliver. "Charlie. I love you." "I love you too, Oliver. Wait," said Charlie. "Is this where you tell me you're gay? If you're coming out, I don't want to kill the moment or anything but, Oliver you know I'm not…"

"No asshole. I just want to tell you that I love you, man. You are my best friend. As your best friend I'm going to choose to be happy for you. What the fuck do I know? If you're in love with this girl, or think you're in love with her who am I to say anything. I'm happy for you. No matter what happens, I'm happy for you because you are one of the greatest guys on earth and you deserve to be happy."

"What the fuck is wrong with you Oliver? Are you sure you're not coming out or something? You can tell me if you are. I'll still be your friend."

"My mom is right. Life is short Charlie. We only get one shot here. We need to live this thing. Who cares if she doesn't love you back? Who cares? It doesn't even matter. Maybe she will be your first wife. Maybe you will have kids together. Maybe you already made one. Who knows? What matters is you're living. I'm living. We're doing this thing."

"Dude, I'm starting to get really worried about you. Did you take something I don't know about? Now is a good time to tell me."

"Charlie, next time I start to feel sorry for myself I want you to hit me."

"Like in the face?" said Charlie.

"I don't know, if you really have to. The shoulder would probably be fine though," said Oliver. "Thank you though, for real Charlie. For being a good friend."

The shadows of the trees had crept all the way across the yard and were about half-way up the trees on the other side as Oliver and Charlie walked towards the house where everyone else was gathering for supper.

"I don't know what I would have done without you, Oliver. You've been my friend since we were kids, most of the time my only friend.

Even though you were always smarter than me, it never seemed to matter. I love you too, Oliver. I really do."

"Are you coming out on me?" said Oliver, smiling and giving Charlie a little shove, "I'd still be friends with you if you were."

"Hey, I almost forgot," said Charlie. "I came to get you because Megan and Star want to go see some of Star's old high school buddies after dinner."

They were greeted in the house by the whole family when they came in for dinner. Star's sister had returned from her abalone hunt and was bubbly and radiant as any healthy 17 year old girl. Oliver liked Taylor. Not the way he suspected Charlie probably did, but she was a good kid. He thought that, before he came on this trip, he would have guessed that the child of a family who grows pot would be different, or a bad kid or something. Her and Star seemed like two well rounded, smart individuals. He felt a little bad for even thinking otherwise.

Star was right about her mom's vegetarian lasagna, it tasted like it had love baked in, and meat. Bill told stories about surfing all over the world. Taylor told all about her abalone hunt earlier that day, and Mel cooked some fresh abalone. Oliver wasn't a huge fan of the meat, it was kind of rubbery and tasted like the sea smelled, but the shells were pretty cool. The native west coasters seemed to love it.

"Star said we might be able to go surfing in the morning," said Charlie.

"Well," said Bill. "We were planning on going surfing, for sure. We've got some extra boards I can throw in the truck."

"Is it hard?" said Charlie.

"Well, it depends on what you think hard is?" said Bill. "It takes a lot of practice. I don't expect that you will go out tomorrow and actually do a lot of what you may think of as surfing. There are a lot of forces acting on you all at once. It takes a little bit to get a feel for it. Luckily, the swells are supposed to be relatively calm tomorrow morning. It'll be a good day to give it a shot."

"Oliver, are you going to try?" said Charlie.

"Not sure," said Oliver. "I've never been a big fan of water."

Charlie punched Oliver in the shoulder.

"Ouch, what did you do that for?"

"You told me to," said Charlie, smiling.

"Dude, that's not exactly what I told you," said Oliver.

"Close enough," said Charlie.

"So a couple of my friends from school want to go to Garberville tonight," said Star. "It's the big town around here. I guess I didn't really ask if you wanted to go," she said, winking at Oliver. "You could stick around here and hang out with Wild Bill and Mel, if you want."

"I'm in," said Charlie.

"Yeah, sounds like fun," said Oliver.

18.5

At night the roads seemed narrower and hillier than they did on the way in. Charlie and Megan used the time, and the dark to get to know each other better. Every so often, the occupants of the front seat could hear a kind of, slurping noise, from the back seat, generated by the intense make-out session.

"So we're meeting up with your high school friends?" said Oliver.

"Yeah, my best friend from high school, Willa, and her husband, Mark. All three of us have known each other since we were little. They have actually been dating since the eighth grade. They got married a year out of high school."

"Are they growers too?" said Oliver.

"Yes," said Star. "About that. If you get into casual conversation with someone around here, don't ask them what they do for a living. It's not polite. A lot of people around here are suspicious and pretty paranoid about stuff like that. If people know me you would be fine, but not everyone is going to know me."

"Got it," said Oliver.

Oliver rolled down his window, partly to get some fresh air, partly hoping the wind noise would drown out the sounds coming from the back seat. The air was cool, but not cold. It smelled deeply of pine forest, and every once in a while there seemed to be a slight whiff of, marijuana or was it a skunk somewhere some distance off the road?

"You talked to your mom this afternoon?" said Star. "How is she? Is she okay? I'm sorry, I shouldn't..."

"No, it's okay," said Oliver. "It's weird, I talk to her and she sounds fine. She sounds normal."

"What kind of cancer does she have?" asked Star.

"I'm not even sure. She doesn't say. She just says its terminal. Like there is no choice. She's talked about chemotherapy, but only to say that she's not going to do it. Like she's giving up or something. She doesn't even want to fight it."

"I'm sorry, Oliver," said Star. "That must be hard for you."

"I guess, yeah... I don't really know how to feel about it. I try to tell her that I want her to fight it, I want her to live, but she doesn't listen to me. There isn't anything I can do. She acts like her work here on earth is done. Like the only thing she was put here for was to have my brother and I and raise us, and now she's done. She doesn't even seem afraid to die."

"Maybe she's not. Is she religious?"

"No, I've never been to a church with her, ever. She never talked to us about any of that kind of stuff growing up. I guess she grew up Catholic, and even went to a Catholic school when she was a kid. From the way it sounds the nuns were pretty mean. She decided that she didn't want anything to do with it pretty early. She's really stubborn. If she gets an idea in her head, she goes with it, and won't let it go. I wish she would have made up her mind to become a millionaire when I was a kid. If she would have got it in her head, I'm pretty sure she would have made it happen."

"I don't know if it helps, but dying is part of the natural cycle of things," said Star.

"What the hell is the natural cycle? We naturally built machines and hospitals and invented medicines. They didn't come from the sky handed down to us. We made them, right? We didn't just wake up one day and the machines, or the medicines were here for us to use. It was a development cycle that's been going on for hundreds or thousands of years. Is the natural cycle now to try and keep ourselves alive? Try and survive as long as we can?"

"To be fair, and I only say this to play the devil's advocate, you and I did just get born into this world of machines and medicine. It wasn't always this way. I think we take it for granted, because for us, it has always been this way," said Star.

"But people have always had a survival instinct right? We've always wanted to stay alive? That's why our species is still here. Because we are survivors. I know I'm scared to die. I'm not even afraid to say it. I'm scared shitless. Who knows what's going to happen next. Is it just over after this? All I know is that I want to live as long as I can."

"Doesn't she have the right to want to leave this place naturally? Why doesn't she want to have chemo?"

"It seems so selfish to me," said Oliver. "Like she doesn't even care what I think, or anybody for that matter. When I talk to her it seems like her main concern is that she doesn't want to lose her hair. She would rather die than lose her hair. She could get a wig right? Who cares, it's just hair."

"Maybe she's scared to lose who she is. You know chemotherapy is really painful too. It doesn't always work either. Maybe she really is terminal? Maybe it's so advanced that there isn't much they can do. Has she said how long she has?"

"No, she won't talk about stuff like how long she has. It's so strange. It's like she's not afraid at all. Like she's totally fine with it. It makes me so angry."

"You're her little boy, Oliver. She probably doesn't want you to worry about her," said Star.

"Well, that's not working," said Oliver.

In the distance a haze of lights came over the horizon through the trees, and they came into the little town of Redway. A few minutes farther south on the 101 and they were in Garberville.

They pulled up to a little bar called the Branding Iron Saloon. Oliver didn't quite know what to expect. In his mind he was seeing a bar full of long hairs and tie died shirts, but the street outside was lined with pickup trucks not VW buses. Inside there were a few old long haired men with beards who dressed vaguely like what Oliver might think of as hippie, but most of the crowd looked more like they belonged in a small redneck country town in Wisconsin.

"Star," yelled a girl from across the bar. "Over here."

They crossed the bar.

"Willa," said Star, hugging her tightly. "These are my friends. Megan, Charlie and this is Oliver."

"Like Oliver Twist," said Willa.

"Exactly like Oliver Twist," smiled Oliver.

"Guys," said Star, "this is Willa and her husband Mark."

"What's everybody want?" said Charlie. "First round is on me."

"I'll take a Jack and Coke, and a shot of whiskey," said Oliver.

"Star, what do you want," said Charlie.

"I'm DD tonight, I'll just take a Sprite," said Star.

Oliver took his drink and shot. He put the shot down without hesitation. He followed that by slamming his drink and bellying up to the bar to order another one. He had his second shot in hand by the time Charlie was raising his first shot to make a cheers with the small group. Oliver slammed down the shot and was half way through with his second Jack and Coke by the time everyone else had picked up their first drink.

"Dude," whispered Charlie. "What are you trying to prove?"

"What's that supposed to mean," said Oliver.

"You're putting them down like you're on a mission," said Charlie.

"Are you my mom now?" said Oliver.

"Hey, buddy, just trying to look out for you. I hardly ever see you drink. The way you're going you're setting yourself up to puke."

"I can handle my booze," said Oliver, finishing his second Jack and Coke, and then ordering another.

"Whatever Oliver, you're a big boy," said Charlie.

"Damn right I am," said Oliver. "I can handle my own shit."

10 minutes and 2 more drinks later, Oliver found himself feeling very alone, standing at the bar, and maybe a little tipsy, like he should maybe sit down for the next drink.

"Oliver," said Star. "Willa wants to know who your favorite author is, she's a book junkie."

"John Steinbeck," said Oliver. "The greatest fucking author to ever live. I'm a writer you know. I'm a fucking pirate writer."

"Right on," said Willa. "I like your hat."

"It was a gift," said Oliver. "It was a gift from a man with a name, who shall remain nameless. But he is a great man."

"Okay, Oliver," said Star, "we've been here for like 20 minutes. Are you drunk already?"

"No," said Oliver. "What's that supposed to mean, Star."

"I don't care. I'm just saying. It seems a little soon. We are going to be here for a while."

"My mom told me I have to live. She told me to make the best of my vacation, because if I don't it's my own fault. She told me to swim in the ocean, because one time she had the chance to and she was too scared and she regrets it. And yes I am. I think I'm drunk. And I'm going to get drunk. And I'm drunk already, cause I don't really drink much."

"Star," said a good looking man about Oliver's age, now approaching.

"Ricky, how have you been?" said Star, giving him a hug. "These are my friends from out of town."

"Looks like a pretty crazy crowd you got here. What are you doing later?" said Ricky.

"Not much, we don't really have any plans," said Star.

"You could let these guys make their way back to wherever they came from and come hang out at my place, if you want. We haven't caught up for a while," said Ricky.

"Don't think so," she said. "That ship sailed a long time ago."

"It's been a long time, Star," said Ricky. "You didn't even call to tell me you were going to be in town."

"Hey. She said she wasn't interested," said Oliver. "We were talking. You are interrupting us. She doesn't want to go anywhere with you."

"Oliver," said Star. "I can handle this."

"No," said Ricky. "Let the freak talk. Let him talk all he wants. Nice hat, fuck wad."

"This hat belonged to a General in Napoleon Bonaparte's army. A ship captain," said Oliver.

"It's going to belong to me after I wipe your ass with it, dick weed."

"Why would you want it after you wiped it in my ass?" said Oliver.

"Who the fuck is this guy?" said Ricky. "Are you fucking this freak, Star?"

"Shut up, Ricky. Leave us alone," said Star.

"Yeah, she is," said Oliver. "She fucked me last night, asshole."

"Oliver!" said Star.

Ricky punched Oliver in the face, and Oliver fell backwards over a bar stool. When the argument started Charlie had quietly picked up a pool stick, which he now used to hit the advancing Ricky directly in the center of the chest.

"What the fuck... who the fuck is this," said Ricky.

"Leave him alone," said Charlie, still holding the pool stick, ready to strike again.

A crowd had started to gather at this point. Ricky advanced on Charlie, and Charlie hit him directly in the face with the butt end of the pool stick. Ricky fell back this time, knocking over a barstool on his way down.

"My fucking tooth," shouted Ricky. "You mother fucker. You knocked out my front tooth!" he said standing up, about to charge again, blood now starting to drip from his mouth.

"Leave them alone, Ricky," said Willa's husband Mark.

"Why the fuck are you sticking up for these foreigners, they're a bunch of losers," said Ricky. "Remember when you used to be my best friend? Now you side with these fucking clowns?"

"Dude, you're out of line," said Mark. "No one wants to cause any trouble here."

"Break it up," said the bar tender. "We don't need any more trouble in here. Ricky, leave the kid alone. Try it again and you're out of here, for good this time."

"That dude hit me in the face with a pool cue. Why are you taking their side?" said Ricky.

"You fucking deserved it," said the bartender. "I'm sick of you starting shit, and drawing attention to my bar. It ends now."

"Fuck you Mike. Fuck all of you. I'm over this place anyway. Bunch of fucking pussies," said Ricky grabbing his coat off the back of a chair. He picked a beer bottle off the counter and threw it at a wall across the bar as he walked out the door.

"You're done here, Ricky," said Mike, the bartender. "You're done. You're not coming back this time."

Oliver was still picking himself off the floor, and holding his fast swelling eye. "I'll take a Jack and Coke," said Oliver.

"You get a Coke," said Mike, the bartender. "Hey, you, kid with the pool stick… what are you drinking? It's on me."

"I don't know," said Charlie. "Do you have a Stout?"

"Why does he get a beer and I don't," said Oliver. "I got punched in the face."

"Because, you're an asshole," said Star.

"What did I do?" said Oliver.

"Mike, do you have an ice pack," said Star.

"Yeah, I can probably come up with something," said Mike.

"First off, you told everyone in the bar we fucked last night," said Star.

"I did, didn't I. Sorry about that. I got caught in the moment I guess," said Oliver.

"Here you go kid. This is a towel full of ice," said Mike.

"Thanks," said Oliver, taking the ice and putting it on the side of his face.

"You're drinking like a high schooler," said Star.

"I'm sick of feeling shit," said Oliver. "I just wanted to shut it off and have a good time."

"Well, that plan didn't work, did it?" said Star.

"I guess not," said Oliver.

The drive back to Star's parents' house was pretty quiet. Oliver held the towel on his face and looked at the passing white stripes in the middle of the road as they ticked by, with his one still good eye. He could hear the little sucking noises from the back seat, and every once in a while a quiet whisper, "Not yet, we have to wait."

"Sorry, I ruined your night with your friends," said Oliver.

"You didn't ruin it," said Star. "It was that asshole, Ricky."

"Is he your ex or something?"

"Yeah, we dated in high school. He was a dick back then too."

"Why did you date him then," said Oliver.

"I don't know. I guess I thought he was cool or something. At the time I kind of thought he was this damaged soul, and if I tried hard enough I could fix him. He's not all bad. He had a pretty rough childhood. His dad is pretty hot tempered too."

"Did you love him?"

"I think I did. Well, when I was that age, and he was my first love, I knew I did. I think I loved the idea of love. When we first started dating the way he made me feel was incredible. I felt special in a way that I don't normally feel, unless I'm falling in love. Since he was my first, it was like a drug. It was intoxicating. When I stayed with him, even after he started treating me like everyone else, the reason I stayed was that I hoped, I tried, to get back to that place that I had been at the beginning. I associated that feeling that I got from love, with him. I didn't know back then, that I could have that feeling with others. That sounds totally weird, I know. Have you ever felt like that? Oliver? Are you awake?"

She shook his shoulder gently, and he was fast asleep.

19

Oliver woke up feeling like he had been hit by a bus. His head hurt. He had a hangover, yes, but it was more than that. His face hurt too. He rubbed his good eye and rolled off the couch onto his feet. He didn't remember getting to the couch at the end of the night.

Light was just starting to fill the living area of the house. Bill stood at the island between the kitchen and the living room.

"Good morning, kiddo," said Bill. "How was your night? Looks like you found some trouble."

"I guess you could call it that," said Oliver. "I found Star's ex-boyfriend. Ricky, I think."

"Good old Ricky," said Bill. "I hope he looks worse than you."

"I'm pretty sure Charlie knocked one of his teeth out with a pool stick," said Oliver. "At least that's what they tell me. I was still picking myself off the floor at the time."

"Well good," said Bill. "You know Oliver... I'm not a violent guy by nature. I've been in a few fights, but only when pushed. I like to think of myself as a man of peace and forgiveness. But I tell you what, there were more than a few times when I wanted to hang that Ricky kid from a tree by his short and curlies and leave him there to think about a few things. I never wanted to kill him, but I came close in my mind's eye."

"I don't know how this looks for sure, but from how it feels, it's probably going to leave a mark," said Oliver.

"It's a pretty good shiner," said Bill. "There's a mirror in the bathroom. There's some Tylenol in there too."

Oliver went into the bathroom and glanced in the mirror on the way to taking the longest piss that he thought he had ever taken. Holy shit, he thought. Looking in the mirror he saw himself, his left eye was black and puffy at the bottom and there was a little black even on his eye lid.

He looked at himself. He remembered Jack asking him if he had ever really looked in the mirror. He tried to look at himself now. That is me, he thought. That is my face. That is what everyone who I come into contact with sees of me. Holy shit, this is really who I am. I think I'm okay with that. He looked deep into his eyes, maybe for the first time. He looked past his puffy eye and straight in. This is me, he thought. I am me.

"Oliver," said Charlie. "That's a pretty big black eye."

"I see that, captain obvious," said Oliver, suddenly snapped out of his reverence. "It fucking hurts."

"Can you believe I hit that dude with a pool stick? That was awesome. It was my first bar fight," said Charlie. "Megan thought it was really hot. Dude, we did it again last night."

"Charlie," said Oliver. "You don't have to tell me every time you guys do it."

"Who else am I going to tell," said Charlie.

"You know. She knows. Who else needs to know?" said Oliver.

"Whatever dude. We're going surfing. How cool is that? Get your shit together. We're headed out right now. Everybody is waking up, and we're going."

"I'm coming," said Oliver. "Just give me a minute." He opened the medicine cabinet and found the Tylenol. He took four of them with a few splashes of water he scooped out of the sink with his hands.

When he walked out into the living area, everyone was in the process of getting up and milling around. It seemed like all eyes were looking at him, trying to see his battle wound. No one else mentioned it. He pulled down the hat as far as he could until it was so tight to the top of his eyes he could barely see.

"Hope you like granola," said Star. "That's all my dad will eat for breakfast."

"Yeah, that's fine. I don't normally eat breakfast anyway," said Oliver. He ate a few bites of granola, and milk that didn't taste like the milk he knew. He figured it must be goat's milk, or maybe it had just gone bad. He couldn't finish it.

It was a bright sunny morning, as they followed Wild Bill's truck, loaded with surf boards to Shelter Cove. The sun peaked through the trees more and more as they reached the coast.

When they reached the parking lot of the beach, there were a few other cars there. On the water they could see a couple of people bobbing around out in the distance.

"We're actually running a little late," said Star. "I think dad was going easy on us, since we went out last night. He usually gets up around 4:30 A.M. and is out here on the water by 5."

"The waves don't seem that big," said Charlie.

"Over there they're 6 to 7 feet," said Star. "Here in front of us they're only 2 to 3 feet. This is where we are going to be. My dad and sister will probably be over there."

"Okay, guys and girls," said Bill, getting out of his truck and rounding to the back where the surf boards were poking out of the metal foam covered rack. "These two boards are called long boards. They are for you guys. These will be the easiest to learn on. Star can take you through some of the basics. I have a couple of extra wet suits here. The water is probably colder than you think. Taylor and I are going over there. You guys try and stay over here. These little waves are plenty big for a beginner."

Star ran through the basics with Megan, Charlie and Oliver. She had them practice popping up on the board and finding their center. She told them where to put their feet and where to try and balance their weight.

"Who's first," said Star.

"I'll go," said Charlie, who had already crammed himself into a wet suit.

He looked a little misshapen, but it didn't seem to bother him. Oliver thought he looked a little like he might pop.

"All right," said Star, "let's head out."

They jogged towards the water and jumped in, onto their surf boards. Star graceful and flowing almost as if she were one with the water, Charlie behind her, flailing and trying to keep up. At one point Charlie fell off his board and Star had to turn around to help him back on.

"Have you ever surfed?" said Oliver.

"I tried it once, last time I was here," said Megan. "I can't say that I was any good at it. I think it takes more than one time for most people to get the hang of it. I like snowboarding, but this is way harder. Have you ever tried it?"

"Nope, I've never been in the ocean," said Oliver.

"You've never been in the ocean? What are you waiting for?" said Megan.

"I'll do it," said Oliver. "I've just got to work myself into it."

"Are you scared? It's okay if you are."

"I'm just not a huge fan of water. I grew up on the Mississippi river, in La Crosse. I just never liked going in it. Every time I went in, even when I was really little I pictured myself being swept all the way down to the Gulf of Mexico."

"I grew up in Green Bay, on Lake Michigan. It was a lot smaller than the ocean, but when I was a kid, I didn't really know that. It looked as big as the ocean from the shore. There were a few surfers there too."

"Really? There are surfers on Lake Michigan?" said Oliver.

"A few, I don't know why there aren't more? Probably because the waves are pretty small most of the year. I think I heard something about them being closer together because the lake is narrower than the ocean, but I'm not sure on that."

"How do you feel about Charlie?" said Oliver.

"That's a change of subject," said Megan, smiling. "I like him. He's a good guy. He's fun."

"Do you have fun with a lot of guys?" said Oliver.

"Whoa there Mr. Pirate Writer. I don't know if I like where this is going? I'm not a slut, if that's what you're implying."

"Shit, I'm sorry, no. No, that's not what I'm trying to say," said Oliver. "It's just that he likes you. I just don't want him to get his heart broken that's all."

"I don't know where this is going. You guys are going back to Wisconsin soon, and I'm going back to Oregon. I like Charlie. I'm having fun, and I think he's having fun too."

"Would you date him?" said Oliver.

"I don't know, probably, if we were both in the same place, I think he's pretty awesome. Yes, I think I would," said Megan. "Me? What about you and Star?"

"What about it? I like her," said Oliver. "This whole thing is so crazy. I certainly didn't expect to come out here and meet a girl. Shit, this time last week I didn't even know I was coming out here. That seems like so long ago now. I understand what you mean about the distance thing. I have to be back to school in a week and a half, and I know you guys do too. I'm sorry I brought it up."

"No, it's okay," said Megan. "You're a good friend. You just want the best for Charlie. I look at it like this. We're all just people on this crazy adventure. You and Charlie and me and Star are here now. Our paths are crossing at a time in our lives where we, for whatever reason, are connecting. We all know that our paths are going to separate soon, but as long as we're here lets have fun and travel together. Maybe I'm turning into one of those west coast hippies my dad is afraid of?"

"No, no that's really cool," said Oliver. "I like that. I wish I could have written it down."

"Maybe someday you will," said Megan. "Hey look, Charlie's standing up. And now he's down."

Charlie tumbled into the water and for a few long seconds all they could see was the board bobbing up and down in the waves. Then, hands waving in what from the shore looked like panic, Charlie grabbed onto the board and tried to pull himself on, and tipped over, and tried again, and tipped over. Star who had been sitting on her board with her feet dangling in the water paddled over and tried to give him pointers, but in the end he just paddled back into shore next to his board.

"Oliver, you got to try this," shouted Charlie, as he ran out of the water. "It's way harder than it looks. And the water is pretty cold. It's the end of summer. I thought it was going to be like bath water."

"Are you ready to try it?" said Star.

"I guess so," said Oliver.

"Switch with Charlie. Take that wet suit and see if it will fit you."

Charlie squirmed out of the wetsuit and into a towel on the blanket next to Megan. Oliver slid into the wetsuit, it seemed like it might have actually have been a little stretched out by Charlie, but Oliver couldn't tell for sure, since he'd never been in one. In any case it went on easily.

"You ready Oliver?" said Star. "You have to take the hat off."

"Ready as I'll ever be," said Oliver.

They ran towards the water, ankle deep, the waves washed against them. Knee deep and the waves pushed against them. Star jumped gracefully and landed on her board in stride and paddling. Oliver attempting to follow jumped onto his board and fell off into the water.

The salt water. It was amazing how salty it actually was. People say salt water, but they call so many things names that don't really make sense. He thought it was amazing how salty it actually tasted. He could have gotten back on his board, but instead he just laid there. On his back, looking at the sky, letting the waves carry him up and then down, up and then down.

"Oliver! Oliver are you okay!" Star shouted.

"I'm fine," said Oliver. "I'm just feeling the ocean."

"What! Are you okay?"

"Yes!" shouted Oliver. "I am good."

Part of him wanted to lay there. Just lay there and take it in. That wasn't the part of him though that was starting to get cold.

He stood up, and the water was about waist deep. He positioned the board next to himself and jumped on. Then rolled off the other side. This was harder than it looked. It wasn't like simply hopping onto something. Everything moved.

Okay, he thought, I can do this. He steadied the board and jumped on, almost falling off the other side, then catching himself.

"Paddle," said Star. "Start paddling."

He was already tired, but he started paddling. It was awkward, his arms hit each side of the board and every time he paddled he felt he was in danger of tipping over off into the water. He paddled. He paddled until he reached where Star had paddled to, and was now sitting upright, straddling her board. He wasn't sure if he could do that.

The waves looked taller out here than they did from the shore. It was slightly quieter than it had been at the shore line, since the waves weren't crashing in right next to them.

"Turn your board around and pick a wave. When you pick your wave, start paddling, paddle hard. When you get to the top, lean forward and stand up, like I showed you on the beach."

Oliver thought he saw a wave coming. He started paddling, he arched his back, he popped up and for a second he felt like he might have it, then he tipped off to the left and fell into the water.

The water was almost over his head when the waves were at their lowest point. He steadied his board, and jumped back on, paddled back out to where Star sat, and readied to try it again.

He was getting tired now. With all the activity he wasn't cold though. He picked a wave out that he thought was good. Paddle, paddle, paddle, stand up. Splash.

He wanted this. This was it. Three times. Four times. Star showed him. She paddled, effortlessly popped up onto her board and rode a wave until it looked to Oliver like she might bump into the shore.

One last time. He paddled. Popped up, and boom. He was standing. Holy shit. He was standing. He was going perfectly straight. He felt weird and awkward, but this was it. He rode it almost all the way into the shoreline, until the wave lost momentum and he lost his balance and fell off the side.

"Yay..." said Star. "You did it. You surfed. How was it?"

"Amazing," said Oliver. "Amazing."

"Take your hat back, Captain," said Charlie, when they got back up to the spot on the beach where the other two were sitting. "Nice work, Oliver."

"Very nice, work," said Megan, handing him a lit joint.

Oliver sat down on the blanket that was spread on the beach, and took a long pull from the joint. A drip of water from his hair landed on the middle of the joint and he hoped he hadn't ruined it. He passed it to Star.

To the left he could see Bill and Taylor. They looked at home in the water. Every movement seemed to flow with the water, even as they paddled out and against the current of the waves. They didn't just pop onto the board to catch a wave. It was one fluid motion. They paddled with the wave for a few seconds and they were on top of it. With it. In a flow with the water and nature itself. Their boards were much shorter and they seemed to move faster. They cut left and right and it seemed to Oliver that they were part of the wave.

Bill was with the wave and in the wave, while Taylor seemed to play with the wave. It was almost as if she and the wave were friends. They played a game, it did this and she did that, like two school children on the playground, laughing and playing.

"Do you want to try anymore surfing?" said Star.

"No, I'm good," said Oliver.

"I'm going to go out with my family for a while," said Star.

Oliver sat and watched her run to the water. She dove in with the beauty and grace he had seen earlier. She paddled out.

Megan and Charlie got up and walked by themselves down the beach. Oliver noticed the half smoked joint lying on the longboard. It had gone out where the drop from his hair had landed and was placed there to dry. He picked it up and found a lighter tucked in the folds of the blanket. He smoked it, and watched.

Star joined her sister and father on the waves. There was nothing said between the three, but the communication they shared was palpable. Star picked a wave and paddled into it. Without question, without pause, she became one with the wave. It moved, and she moved, together, as one. It seemed as though there were no separation between her and the wave. They were one thing.

It may have been the most beautiful thing Oliver had ever seen. In that moment he saw joy, and freedom and connectedness all at once. There was a beauty and honesty in the dance he was witnessing, and he decided that in his recognition of it, he had joined in its oneness, its singularity.

20

"It's been great to meet you," said Mel.

"Thanks," said Oliver. "You have a really nice family."

Hugs were given, and they were once again on the road, headed back up the 101 Northbound. Time passed quickly, with talk and laughter.

21

"Holy shit, kid. What happened to your face?" said Jackson.

"It got in the way of my mouth," said Oliver.

"Fuck man. You gotta watch your shit. You need to be able to control yourself. You're gonna stand out like a sore thumb on your way back with that thing on your face," said Jackson.

"Don't worry too much," said Mia. "I can teach him how to put cover up on it. It will barely be noticeable."

"That's not the point," said Jackson.

"When you're doing a job, there is a way in which you need to conduct yourself. This is serious shit. It's not just a surfing vacation at the beach. Yeah, you can do that, but you need to be able to handle that. You got called out."

"He was defending me," said Star.

"Good," said Jackson. "Do that too. But don't get turned into a bitch while doing so. Don't draw attention."

"You're making me wear this fucking pirate hat. You don't think that is going to draw attention?" said Oliver.

"No. For one thing, you're in Humboldt County. People wear all kinds of weird shit here. Wearing something like that is going to make you look more like a local. No tourist kid is going to have the balls to wear something like that. Now you have this fucking shiner on your eye. Now you're the kid with the hat and the big fucking black eye. You take the hat off and you still have the black eye."

"I'm sorry, Jackson," said Oliver. "What more can I say. I got drunk and pissed off the wrong guy. I wish I could say he looked worse than me. Well, actually I think he might have. I'm told that he lost a tooth."

"You hit him back?" said Jackson.

"No, Charlie did," said Oliver. "He hit him in the chest, then in the face with a pool stick."

"You would have done the same for me," said Charlie.

"I was still picking myself up off the floor by the time the guy was getting kicked out," said Oliver.

"He got kicked out and you guys didn't?" said Jackson.

"Yeah, the bartender bought Charlie a drink," said Oliver.

"I may be starting to like you Charlie. Sounds like you are a good guy to have in a pinch. You wouldn't know by looking at you," Jackson laughed. "Look. I don't really give a shit what people think here. Nobody here cares what you look like. The main thing is driving back. When you're going through Utah or Wyoming or Nebraska, they are going to take two good looks at you. With that thing on your face it will be easy to remember, and easy to identify you."

"I'm sorry Jackson," said Oliver.

"It is what it is," said Jackson. "Get good at putting that makeup on. Who was this guy anyway, just some random stranger you pissed off?"

"It was my ex," said Star.

"For fuck sake," said Jackson. "You dumb fucks, I should have known. Well, it's all over but the cryin'. We still have some trimming left, if you guys want to jump in. Tonight we're having a beach party to warm into the event tomorrow night, so get rested up if you need to."

Charlie and Megan went over and joined back in at the trimming table.

"I still need to make some more money before school starts," said Star. "I'm going to do some trimming too, Oliver."

"Don't worry about me," said Oliver. "I'm not sure what I'm going to do yet. I might just relax a little."

Oliver sat down on the couch near Chewy, who had just finished rolling a joint that seemed to Oliver about the diameter of his middle finger.

"You want to light it?" said Chewy.

"I don't know," said Oliver. "I really just wanted to sit down and relax for a while."

"You know who smokes a lot of weed?" said Chewy, seemingly out of the blue.

"You and Jackson?" said Oliver.

"Well, there is that too," said Chewy, lighting the joint. "I was in India a few months ago. They have these Yogis over there. They're these Hindi spiritual guys that they call Sadhu Monks. They give up all connection to ownership. They stop trying to make money. They give up all family ties. They live off only the kindness of others. In search of God. They smoke a ton of hash."

"Do they think the hash makes them more spiritual?" said Oliver.

"They think so. They have many gods. Well, I don't fully understand Hinduism, but I think there are main gods and minor gods. Shiva for example, is a commonly worshiped god and the Sadhu monks I talked to worshiped Shiva as their main god. He is often depicted smoking a chillum, and meditating. They smoke hash to be closer to Shiva, as a way to access the divine."

"What's a chillum?" said Oliver.

"It's this pipe that you don't actually put your mouth to. It's kind of nice really, if you don't want to spread germs. Different guys do it different ways, but you kind of hold it in your hand or between a couple of fingers and make the final leg of the pipe by shaping your hand into a straw. Then draw from your hand. It's a little weird at first, but these guys are experts at it."

"Is weed legal in India?"

"It's not really legal in most places. It's tolerated for the most part. Especially if you're a Yogi. I guess if you're willing to give up all human possessions and desire, you can get away with a lot. In their society they hold these guys in pretty high regard. Here, if a guy lives on the street and begs for his meals, he's considered a parasite. There is no honor in it. Over there, it's something that is aspired to. I met a guy who was very proud that he was the first Sadhu in his family. Like someone here who might be proud that he's the first Catholic priest in his family."

"Are these guys really holy? Do they have the answers?" asked Oliver.

"It depends on what you mean by, 'the answers,'" said Chewy. "I don't think they know everything. They are seeking enlightenment."

"Did you ask them any questions about life?" said Oliver.

"Mostly I just asked them about their stories. I didn't really speak their language, and most only spoke bits and pieces of broken English. None of them turned down a fresh packed chillum though. After a few huge tokes they were pretty happy to talk about almost anything."

"With all that meditating they must know something. Are they enlightened?" said Oliver.

"Hard to say. Some of them probably are. They all have a teacher. A main guy is called a Guru. The Guru teaches all the traditions and most of those guys claim to be enlightened," said Chewy.

"You don't think they actually know things?" said Oliver.

"Lots of people know things. I think they are trying to understand all things. I think that is kind of their goal. I think they know things in a way that they understand to be true. Like most religions, they have a dogma that guides them."

"Do you think they are holy?" said Oliver.

"Yes. I think they are holy. They live with virtue in a way that is sacred to them. Their aim is to live a life entirely dedicated to their gods. The idea is that this will help stop the reincarnation cycle, so when they die they will access the divine."

"Do you believe in reincarnation? Do you think that we are born again on this earth?" said Oliver.

"The Hindus believe in reincarnation. I am not a Hindu, but I think reincarnation is just as probable as life completely ending."

"What do you think happens when we die? Are you religious?" said Oliver.

"I don't know what happens when we die? I know it's one of the few things we all have in common. Every single person on this planet has exactly two things unmistakably common. They will all be born, and they will all die. That's the way it has always begun, and ultimately, that's the way it will all finish. As far as the religious thing, if you nailed me to a tree and made me proclaim a religion I would probably say I'm a Buddhist more than anything. I grew up Catholic and the hypocrisy and ridiculousness of it all pretty much turned me off to religion for many years. I think religion can be a slippery slope. Collective belief is a powerful tool. Very nasty things are done in the name of true belief."

"But do you believe in an afterlife? Do you believe that you go to a better place when you die?" said Oliver.

"Like I said… I think belief is a funny thing. I don't think you have to believe anything. Things will happen even if you don't believe they will and things don't always happen just because you believe they are going to. Belief and truth are not always in agreement when looked at through the lens of reality. We are in a cycle. The cycle was here before us and the cycle will continue even after we are gone from what we know to be our life as it is now. We are in a cycle, and as far as we know, we are on the very cusp of it—the very leading edge of existence as we know it. No living human has ever lived past this very moment in time, right now. And it has always been that way, just as far back in time as we have realized that we will someday die. One thousand generations ago, they had the very same feelings we do about being in this second on the leading edge of time."

"Here is the thing. My mom has cancer. I don't even know what kind, she won't tell me, and she won't tell me how long they think she has. She isn't going to get treatment. She is just going to die," said Oliver.

"Are you asking if I think it's okay to die? Then the answer is yes. Are you upset because you think she isn't thinking about you?"

"No. She can't just die. That's why we have doctors. Her life will just be over. She's just giving up," said Oliver. "I mean yes. I don't want her to die. She's the only parent I have. I guess I think she's being selfish."

"Have you told her this?" said Chewy.

"I've tried. She's stubborn. Once she gets something in her mind, it's almost impossible to get it out," said Oliver.

"You know in some cultures, like the Sadhu's and Buddhist monks, dying is not a bad thing—if you're at the right place in your life. If you have achieved enlightenment, death is okay. They are not afraid of it," said Chewy.

"My mom's not a monk or a holy person at all. I'm not sure if she's stepped foot in a church in her adult life, except maybe for weddings."

"You don't have to be holy in the traditional way. Honestly, if my mom were not afraid of death, I would be happy for her. My mom is afraid of everything. She is afraid of life. She is afraid of her husband, she is afraid I will never come to visit. She is afraid of the next door neighbor. She is afraid to go to the store by herself," said Chewy.

"My mom has never really been afraid of anything that I know of, but I don't know if that that makes her a better person," said Oliver.

"Is she a good person?" said Chewy.

"She's the best, most selfless person I know," said Oliver. "But what do I know? I don't even really know that many people, I mean really know them."

"Sounds like she has self-confidence. To me, that is one of the best virtues when done properly. When done properly, it means you can see beyond your ego, and do things based on what needs to be done. If I had the power to give someone one thing, I think I would give them confidence. I think a lot of people would choose to give happiness. Happiness is important, but without a solid foundation, it is empty. It comes and goes. Happiness is a gift. Confidence is an inner strength.

"I think I might choose happiness, if given the choice. I've never really thought about it though," said Oliver.

"With a proper confidence, you don't have to be happy all the time. Lack of ecstatic happiness isn't necessarily sadness. If you were perpetually happy, you might not be able to feel sadness properly. I think a lot of the junkies heroin and crystal meth produce are related to a perpetual search for happiness. Always trying to reach that happy place. That place where nothing else matters in the world and everything is right. Ignoring the fact that their life has fallen apart. When they come down, one of the reasons it's so hard is that they have neglected all the sadness, all the things that caused the sadness. The world may be literally crumbling around them and all they want to do is get back into that little pocket of ecstasy."

"Don't you think weed is like that? You guys smoke a lot of it," said Oliver.

"I'm not going to say that weed is the magic drug, but it is completely different than meth or heroin. You don't lose yourself to it. Nothing changes except your mind set. It is much more retrospective. That's why it sometimes makes you paranoid. It makes you think about the shit in your life that is bothering you. If you use it properly, it can be a great asset. Not everyone uses it properly, but that is not the weeds fault. The knife in the hands of a madman and a knife in the hands a surgeon is the same knife. Weed in the hands of a madman, might make him chill out a little," said Chewy.

"I don't want my surgeon to be smoking weed," said Oliver.

"That's where the confidence comes in," said Chewy. "You don't need to, and shouldn't, smoke weed all the time. You see me smoking a lot of weed. Yes, I like to partake. It's harvest season, time to celebrate. I've got no place to be. No one to practice surgery on. Except maybe you," smiled Chewy.

"I just don't want to lose my mom. I think that's normal right?" said Oliver.

"Oliver, that's about the most normal thing you've said since you've been here," said Chewy.

"Holy shit," said Jackson. "Oliver, I don't think I've ever seen anyone make Chewy talk that much all in one stretch. Not even me."

"You were listening?" said Oliver.

"Only for a while," said Jackson. "I didn't say anything, because I was amazed."

"Oliver," said Chewy. "I don't have all the answers. I'm just as fucked up as you think you are. I'm just a little older, and I think about shit. That's all, no more, no less. One thing I can tell you that I feel is important, that isn't really a belief, but a thing that I have come to try and understand—I think we are all one. We think we are different people, and in most obvious respects we certainly are different. We all look at the world through the lens that we are given, and that lens is shaped and developed as we grow. Deep down I think that we are all the same though. I think I am the same as you, with my own perspective. You are the same as your mother, but you were born into a different body. That's why compassion works. When we get rid of all the layers on top, we are all the same in the core. How we use our core, or bury it, is up to us. I don't know what we are, and that part doesn't really matter. We are something inside this meat body shell. We walk around in this thing that is like a biological space suit, designed and evolved for life on this planet. The body is just the body. When the body dies, it is the end of the body. Maybe not the end of that thing that is inside it."

"Why are we here?" said Oliver.

"I don't know," said Chewy.

"How do we figure it out?" said Oliver.

"I don't know that either. I know in Buddhism for example, the most important thing is to try and understand yourself."

"What good does that do?"

"If you know you, you will know me. If you know me you can know everyone," said Chewy.

"That's fucked up," said Jackson. "Just take care of your shit, kid. That's all you need to know to be a man."

"That's true too," said Chewy. "Taking care of all your shit, is a great place to start."

"I don't think I get it," said Oliver.

"If it was as easy as hearing some words, we would all get it," said Chewy.

"What if I don't remember all that stuff you said?"

"You don't have to remember it. You just have to feel it. You feel it by living it," said Chewy.

"All right," said Jackson. "Let's put this kid to work before you fuck him up too badly. Come with me, Oliver."

"He's not fucking me up," said Oliver. "I asked. I want to know."

"I'm just trying to cut the serious shit. It's making my head hurt," said Jackson.

"He has a weak head," said Chewy.

"Fuck off brother," said Jackson. "I will mentally drop kick your ass."

"I will fuck your mom," said Chewy.

"All right you got me," laughed Jackson. "Come over here, Oliver. I need some help with something in the garage."

21.5

Oliver had never been in the garage, but he knew that's where Jackson always brought the bags of weed from. He assumed that's where the strong odor came from. As the door opened he realized that it wasn't entirely from the bags stored in there.

Inside the lights were bright. It was packed from wall to wall and about chest high with plants. There was one walkway down the center, and little branches of walkways in between. He could see there had been masking tape laid on the floor in lines that looked as though that was where the rows of pots were supposed to go.

"Holy shit," said Oliver. "Is this where you grow all your plants?"

"Not quite," said Jackson. "This is just the research and development location. Most of the actual growing now a days happens outdoors. These are the mothers. In here we cross lines, to see which plants will produce, and how well. This is where new strains are developed. See this row here? This is a cross between Purple Mamba and Juicy Fruit. I'm not sure how well it's going turn out. The buds smell really nice, but see this, they're all pretty wispy. I like the buds to be denser."

"How did you learn all this stuff?" said Oliver.

"Just picked it up over the years," said Jackson. "When I'm interested in something, it comes pretty easy. So here's the thing. My drip irrigation system took a shit this morning. I need a new pump for it. Even if I get the pump it might take a while to fix. They need water now. I'm going to run and get the pump, but my girls are getting a little dry. I'll pay you to water them."

"I'll water them, you don't have to pay me," said Oliver.

"Of course I do," said Jackson. "Here, the bucket is right here, and the water spigot is here. I'll be back in about two hours with the parts."

"How much do they need?" said Oliver. "I'm clueless about plants."

"Just use your best judgment," said Jackson. "Sometimes they like to be talked to. I'll be back in a while."

"Talk to them? Like how?" said Oliver. "Are you serious?"

"Sure. Tell them whatever you want," said Jackson. "Tell them they're dirty cunts, or tell them one day they will grow up to be beautiful aliens, whatever you want."

"Does it help them?" said Oliver.

"It might help you, kid. The plants may tell secrets, but they never repeat anything you say. All right, don't give them too much water. I gotta go."

"Wait," said Oliver, but Jackson was already out the door.

The room was brightly lit, and smelled strongly of pungent marijuana. Oliver had never seen growing plants like this in real life. He had seen them in movies. In the movies, the leaves didn't glisten in the light. If he looked really close, the leaves had little hairs that caught the light. The buds had little crystals, and if he looked closely they seemed to shimmer in the bright white of the grow room.

He grabbed the water pail, and the cup that was sitting next to it, filled the pail and went to the first plant.

"How much water do you need?"

The plant didn't reply. The soil seemed really dry, and some cracks had started to form on the surface. He added a cup full, and the soil soaked it up in seconds, seeming to ask for more. So he gave it another cup full.

"I don't know anything about plants, you know."

The second plant said nothing. This one didn't seem quite as dry. There were no visible cracks in the soil. The surface was dry but not as bad as the first. He gave it one cup and it didn't seem to soak in as fast as the previous plant.

"I hope that's enough, friend. Jackson told me not to give you too much."

He went down the rows in this way. One cup, two cups, three cups, depending on what the plant looked like it needed—talking to them.

"You know… I thought it would be funny to talk to you. It's not hard at all. It seems like it should be silly to talk to a plant, but it doesn't feel that way. I think it would be silly if someone saw me. Or maybe not? Maybe it's the bright lights, or the heat, but for some reason it feels like you can hear me. Do you answer questions? If I ask you something can you answer me? Is that a no? That's okay. You are very beautiful."

He looked up and saw a bud the size of his fist.

"You are the biggest. You have some big buds, my friend. Does big make you strong?"

"That one is called Mighty Dragon."

"Holy shit. Oh, hello Star. Fuck, how long have you been listening to me?"

"Not long," said Star.

"I'm not sure how much I need to add to these guys. I'm just guessing."

"I think you are doing well. I was looking for you, and Chewy said Jackson had you in here watering the plants."

"I must look crazy talking to the plants, Jackson told me to."

"It doesn't seem crazy at all. I used to talk to our plants all the time. They say it helps them. I'm sure it's just a myth, but who knows. The only time they ever answered me was when I was eating mushrooms," Star smiled.

"What are mushrooms like?"

"It's hard to say. It's different every time, and it's different for everyone. Most of the time for me it's very playful. It can be serious too. When I was going through some hard times and ate them alone it was pretty serious. It made me look at a lot of things that I was doing wrong. I think they help. But like I said, it's different for everyone," said Star.

"When it was serious was it scary?" said Oliver.

"Sort of. Yeah, I would say it was scary. I would not suggest doing them alone, unless you have had some experiences with them before. If you do them, your first few times should be with other people you trust, and preferably people who have done them before. If you start to go in a negative direction, someone with experience can help guide you through it."

"You said they can be playful? What did you mean by that?"

"It's hard to say. You're going to think I'm crazy, but they kind of talk to me sometimes. I know it sounds messed up. There is probably something in my brain that is activated and doing something that was caused by the interaction with the plant, but it seems like it's coming from outside of me. It's a funny thing. It's like I can see the nature of things. Sometimes, like if I'm at a festival with a large group of people, I can see who people really are, in the moment anyway. Different people give off different vibes and I am super aware of them. I have this game that I play sometimes, where I walk through the crowd and feel the different energy changes. I just sort of wander around until I find a really positive place, then I'll just hang out there for a while. Then maybe I'll go looking for a different vibe."

"I would really like to try them," said Oliver.

"What I have been told is, 'don't be too eager.' If you desire them too much, they seem to be less predictable in how they are going to act. I don't know how it works or anything, that's just what I've been told."

"That's weird, how can you want to take something and not be eager?"

"I don't know. I think it means if you're eager you're more likely to take too many because you really want to see something you think is going to be cool, or you think they are going to help you in a certain way, so you take too much. That's just what I've heard from a few people who are way more experienced with them than me."

"How many times have you done them?" said Oliver.

"I think 6 or 7. It's not really something you can get addicted to. There was a time when I did them a few times in a pretty short period, but they kind of let you know if you're doing them too much. They are really cool, but I don't think you should do them too much, or too often. If I do them once or twice a year that's plenty for me."

"Do you know where I can get any?"

"Oliver, I came in here hoping you would kiss me," Star smiled. "Would you rather do that or ask more questions?"

22

"You fuckers," said Jackson. "Looking sexy Star."

"Shit," said Oliver, trying to cover Star the best he could with his naked body.

"Get out of here, Jackson," said Star. "We are busy."

"How was I supposed to know you two were in here fucking, I thought I was paying Oliver to water these plants," Jackson grinned.

"I'll get them finished, I promise," said Oliver.

"I got the new pump. I'm still going to have to install it, and get the system back up. We're all going to the sundown bonfire in about an hour, so try and get these girls finished up."

Oliver rolled over to his back on the blanket they had found, and looked up at the brightly lit ceiling of the garage.

"Sorry about that, Star," said Oliver.

"It's not your fault," laughed Star. "We were fucking in the garage in the middle of the afternoon. What did we expect? It's not the first time Jackson's seen people making love."

"I know, it's just a little embarrassing," said Oliver.

"Only if you let it be," said Star.

"You want to help me water these plants," said Oliver.

"Sure."

They put their clothes back on, and Oliver was almost surprised that he didn't feel ashamed of his body. He remembered being ashamed when in the shower by himself as a teenager. He looked at

Star putting her clothes back on and wanted these moments to freeze in time.

"Okay," said Star, wiggling her pants back on. "You carry the bucket and I'll work the cup. We have 6 rows left."

"Got it," said Oliver.

They worked fast. Oliver didn't feel like he was doing much, just moving the bucket a couple feet every few minutes. Star quickly, and with great care, watered each plant.

"You are a big girl," she said to the plant in front of her.

"Why do you call all of them girls?" said Oliver.

"They are all female plants. The females create nicer buds, and if there is no male around, they won't produce seeds."

"How can you tell that they're female?"

"You look right here, in the forks of these branches," said Star. "The male has balls. For real. Well, not really balls, it's a little flower bud looking thing. The female has this pointy thing here, called a Calyx with little hairs coming out of it called Pistils."

"Don't you need a male and a female to breed?"

"Not always," said Star.

"You can take clippings of the branches and sprout them, and make an exact clone of the plant."

"That's amazing," said Oliver.

"Plants rule the world," smiled Star. "There, last row finished."

When they stepped back out of the garage it felt to Oliver like they were stepping into another dimension. The bright lights, and silence of the grow room had been replaced by the fading light of the late afternoon coming through the windows, and laughter and conversation coming from the trim crew.

"Alright everyone," said Mia. "If we are going to make sunset, we're going to have to leave soon."

Everyone began to gather in the living room.

"We are going to Moonstone beach," said Mia. "Oliver, can you drive your van. We should be able to get everyone in two vehicles.

The less the better. There are already some kids down there putting the fire together. Oliver, we will follow you. Get on the 101 and head south, you'll see the signs."

They split everyone between two vehicles, Oliver's van and Mia's Subaru. Oliver led the way.

"Why do you think they are having me lead?" said Oliver.

"Probably want to keep an eye on you, and make sure you and Star aren't trying to do it while driving," said Charlie.

"Fuck off," said Oliver.

The trip was short. It only seemed like a few miles. They pulled off the highway and followed the road down to the beach parking lot.

The sun was just over the water as everyone got out of the cars and headed down to the beach. There were close to 20 people already down there, and several more cars coming into the parking lot.

In the open area of the beach, to the right of some large rock outcroppings, they had made a fire pile. It was very large, and stacked into a tee-pee shape. Some of the logs in the fire looked 10 to 12 feet long and had large stumps on the bottom.

"That is a huge fire pile," said Oliver.

"It's mostly drift wood," said Star. "These guys that were here before us must have collected it from up and down the beach."

"Star, how are you?" said a girl with long brown hair.

"Hello, Donna," said Star. "I'm good, how are you?"

"I'm great. Love these bonfires, they're so exciting," said Donna.

"Donna, this is my friend Oliver," said Star.

"Oh, hello Oliver. I love your hat," said Donna.

"Thanks," said Oliver.

"How much cooler, can this place get?" said Charlie.

"It's pretty amazing," said Oliver. "It's almost too good to be true."

"Whatever, Oliver. You always find a way to make it seem shitty," said Charlie.

"That's not even true," said Oliver. "Besides, I'm not making it seem shitty. I'm just a realist, if it seems too good to be true it probably is not true."

"Nothings perfect man," said Charlie. "Never will be. Just go with it."

"Go fuck yourself," smiled Oliver.

"That's the spirit," laughed Charlie.

Everyone began to congregate around the unlit fire. The sound of the ocean rolling in and out mixed with the buzz of conversation. The bottom of the big round sun in the distance began to slip into the ocean, at the horizon.

"Gather around everyone," said Mia, in a loud voice that seemed to carry on the breeze. "Thank you everyone for coming this evening. Thank you mother earth for providing a bountiful harvest. I hope to see all of you tomorrow night. Be safe and I love you all."

Someone passed Oliver a joint. He accepted and inhaled as he looked across the water at the large globe of a sun. It was giant and round. He couldn't believe how fast it went down once it got close to the horizon. Half way then a quarter. Someone else passed a joint and he took a deep drag, still staring at the round, orange, yellow, red orb in the sky. Then another joint, and another. He found himself standing alone, water almost touching his toes. The sun on its final slip into the water, a split second flash of white light hit him directly between the eyes.

Boom. The bonfire behind him roared to life the exact moment the sun sank into the deep. Then the drums began. Then the howling. 50 maybe 60 people now around the roaring bonfire, howling and yipping joyfully for life.

"Owwoooow... Yip yip owwwooowwooo..." howled Oliver. "This is amazing," he shouted.

"I know," shouted Star.

"I feel alive," said Oliver. He grabbed Star around the waist, looked up to the night sky and gave a huge wail.

"What the fuck is this? A cult?" shouted Charlie.

"I don't think so," shouted Megan, smiling from ear to ear. "It's a celebration. They do it every year. Let me here you scream. I want your best primal scream."

"AAAAhhhhh…   AAAAAhhhhAAAhhhhaah… AAhhhhhhhhaaaaaaaaaaahAAHHHH…"

"Amazing right?" said Megan.

"Wow," said Charlie. "I think I broke it."

After 10 or 15 minutes, the howling and wailing subsided, but the drums remained.

Oliver, Star and Charlie all sat a safe distance from the fire.

"Hello," said Mia, sitting down next to Oliver. "How is it for you?"

"Amazing," said Oliver. "I've never experienced anything like it."

"We started this a few years ago with just a handful of people. It's grown quite a bit. It's growing, like a large family," smiled Mia.

"Thanks for everything," said Oliver.

"There is nothing to thank me for," said Mia. "All this isn't me, it's all of us."

"No, I mean everything this week," said Oliver. "For being so cool. Letting me into your house and hanging out and all."

"I know what you meant, Oliver," Mia smiled. "You're a good person, Oliver. You have a bright soul."

"What does that mean? Can I talk to you? Alone?" said Oliver.

"Of course," said Mia.

The two of them walked away from the fire and towards the water's edge. It was cool away from the fire after getting somewhat used to the radiant warmth. In the distance where the sun had once been was now dark. There was no clear line where the darkness of the ocean left off and the darkness of the sky began. Way out in the distance a single light blinked on and off.

"What is that light out there?" asked Oliver.

"It's a ship," said Mia. "Probably a fishing boat."

"Mia, my mom told me to figure out why we are here," said Oliver.

"Did she want to know for her, or for you?"

"What do you mean?" said Oliver.

"Did she ask you because she was questioning it, or because she wanted you to understand it?"

"What's the difference?" said Oliver.

"Oliver, there is no one answer, and it wouldn't mean the same to everyone even if there were an answer. What I meant was did she ask it because she was wondering, or because she wanted you to think about the nature of it?"

"I just don't know why she thinks it's okay not to fight her cancer. What in the world does understanding the meaning of all this have to do with wanting to stay alive? If life is worth living, if it's worth it to be here, why give up? Why is it okay just to leave everyone you love?"

"It's very natural to feel the way you do."

"Yeah, but is it natural to just be okay with dying, and not caring about the people you leave behind?"

"Oliver, we have been around in the human form for many thousands of years. How many people do you think have died in that time?"

"I don't know, billions, trillions, I guess," said Oliver.

"All of them," said Mia. "Every person who has ever lived, before our current time line, this thing we call the present, has passed away."

"Then why isn't it easier?" said Oliver.

"We have survival built in. We have instincts that have served us well through the generations. If we didn't have a survival instinct, we as humans may have gone away long ago."

"So we die. I get it. We want to survive. I know that too. That's what I was trying to say before. What happened to her survival instinct? Why doesn't she care if she dies?"

"How do you know that she doesn't care?"

"I guess I don't know that exactly. Except that she's just going to let it happen. She's just going to let it take her. She acts like losing her hair is worse than death."

"I couldn't begin to tell you what your mom is feeling, Oliver. But if I were to guess I would say, I think she is trying to tell you that it is okay to let her go."

"That's bullshit!" said Oliver.

"What do you think this life is for, Oliver?"

"I don't know. I don't know. I just don't know."

"Think...if someone came to you, with a deep question. They came to you with an honest intent to know. Forget about your current circumstance. Tell me as you would tell them."

"I don't know. I feel like what you want me to say is that, we are born, we live, we are supposed to live well, and then we die with all who love us around us in a bed, and drift off into the sunset."

"I am the one asking you, Oliver. I'm not asking for what you think I want to hear. I am asking what you think."

"I think there has to be some sort of meaning to all this. Otherwise what's the point? Does it matter? Does it matter what I think? It just happens. Sometimes it just happens to us, like there is nothing we can even do about it. Sometimes it's like we can control it. In the end we will be who we are, we will see what we see, we will do what we do and it will be over. I would like to think that what I do and how I act will matter."

"Does what you think and do matter?" asked Mia.

"I don't know. It feels better to be loved than not. When I treat the people better I feel more love. I guess that's something."

"So what is being alive for you? What's the point of life for you, Oliver?"

"Being here, I guess. Learning all this stuff. Feeling and seeing all this stuff."

"Your mom is in a different part of her life," said Mia. "The same in that she is feeling all of these things you are talking about, but different in what she is feeling. Right now, you are feeling the breeze from the ocean on your face. She is feeling something different. You are feeling confused by what life is telling you. She is being clearly told that life is nearing an end for her. This life is coming to the natural conclusion that we will all realize."

In the background Oliver heard the beating of the drums. It seemed like many ages ago that he was back in Wisconsin. The cool ocean breeze filled him with that now unmistakable smell of ocean.

They walked back to the fire in silence. Mia went one way, and Oliver sat cross-legged by himself a safe distance from the fire. Someone handed him a drum.

"Here take this. I'll be back for it," the man said, and walked into the darkness.

Oliver looked at it in the light of the fire. It was very beautiful. It looked as though it may have been hand carved? The skin was stretched tightly over the top, and hair remained on the edges, but the surface of the drum was smooth and well worn.

He picked it up. He sat it on his lap, and started beating it. Boom botta boom batta boom botta boom... To the rhythm of the circle. Then harder, boom botta boom batta boom botta boom... He found that if he put it between his legs and lifted the bottom off the sand several inches, it was louder. Boom botta boom batta boom botta boom...

The sound of the drums that before were outside of him now engulfed him. He was in it. This was real. It felt very real. Boom botta boom batta boom botta boom...

All around the camp fire he could see people talking and drinking beers, smoking and laughing. He was the drum. He was the drum. He became the rhythm. Boom boom batta botta boom boom botta batta boom... As the rhythm evolved, he evolved.

The man who owned the drum came back from the darkness, and sat next to Oliver. Looking at the people and the fire, he sat silently, and lit a joint. He sat, and watched and smoked.

Boom boom thump thump batta batta batta... Boom boom thump thump batta batta batta...

Oliver opened his eyes as the man next to him passed him the joint. He stopped beating his drum, and the drumming continued. He inhaled deeply, and closed his eyes as he passed the joint back. He fell back in and caught the rhythm.

"Oliver, there you are," said Charlie, sitting down next to him. The man passed Charlie the joint.

"Oliver, Charlie," said Star, as Star and Megan came to sit alongside them.

"Hey guys," said Sam and Rex, and pretty soon everyone in the trim crew were sitting around them.

Oliver closed his eyes, beat the drum, and smiled. There was laughter and talk all around him. The flames licked the sky, and embers floated to the stars. Boom batta boom batta boom boom boom batta... A joint came by and Oliver paused in his drumming to inhale. The beat stopped. Five seconds. Ten seconds. Fifteen seconds. The beat was silent. He began again, and the beat continued. Boom boom botta boom boom batta boom boom boom...

23

Oliver woke up lying next to Star. Charlie and Megan were sleeping on the floor, on top of a couple of yoga mats. Oliver realized that they had taken all the good covers and left Star and Oliver with only a sheet. Star's bare breast was exposed and Oliver covered it up.

He lay on his back and looked up at the ceiling. Was he ever going to get back to Wisconsin? Did he ever want to? This may be one of the last times he would wake up next to her. He smelled the unmistakable smell of bacon. Oliver made sure Star was fully covered then slipped out of bed and put on his hat.

He walked down the hall and through the living room, careful not to step on the sleeping bagged bodies of the other trimmers who were scattered among the floor. The blinds were drawn and though it was light outside, the living room was very dim. He almost stepped on Jason the trimmers head.

"Good morning, Oliver," said Jackson, as Oliver stepped into the kitchen. "How the fuck are you this fine morning?"

"Good," said Oliver, still struggling to decide how he was actually feeling about things.

"You my friend need to pay more attention while driving," said Jackson.

"What, where did that come from?" said Oliver.

"Last night on the way to the beach, when you left our road you didn't signal. Then when you exited the off ramp for Moonstone, you didn't signal."

"You were the only one behind me," said Oliver. "You knew where I was going. I thought you were the only one around."

"No excuse. Cops don't always sit in the open. They are always there. You always use your turn signals. You always obey the rules of the road. No exceptions."

"Jackson, if I had something in the car I would have…"

"No, Oliver. You always obey the rules of the road. Get used to it. Always act as though you have something to hide. You get more comfortable with it that way."

"Fine, I will always obey the rules of the road," said Oliver.

"Don't fucking take this lightly kid," said Jackson, in a more serious tone than Oliver had ever seen in him. "Look at me. You fucking look at me… Straight in the eye. This is not a fucking joke. You get that. This is for real."

"Yes," said Oliver. "Yes, yes, I get it. I got it."

"They will put you in a fucking cage. They will take everything that you hold dear. They will feed you to the lions, because you have the audacity to carry a plant in your car. It is some serious shit you are doing my friend. You need to know this. Your brother sent you out here because he lost his nerve, and he is still addicted to the money it brings in. You need to know that too. I am not going to send you out on that road with a carload of my shit to get busted with. You can leave here any time you want, but I am not going to send you out of here with an ounce of this shit until you are fucking ready. You need to know that. If you need to get back to school and that day hasn't come yet, that's your call. If you leave here and something unspeakable goes down, I do not want this shit to come back on me. If you leave here with my weed, if you get busted, I do not want this shit to come back on me. Do I make myself crystal fucking clear?"

"Yes," said Oliver.

"How do you want your fucking eggs?" said Jackson.

"Easy over," said Oliver.

"Your eye is starting to look better."

"Thanks, yeah the swelling is pretty much gone down. There's still the black spot."

"I'll make sure Mia teaches you how to use makeup to cover that up," said Jackson.

"Good morning gentlemen," said Jason the trimmer, stretching and stepping into the kitchen.

"How do you want your eggs?" said Jackson.

"With no chicken in it," said Jason. "Just kidding. I'll go sunny side up. If you got them."

"I can make that happen," said Jackson.

"How are you feeling this morning, my young friend," said Jason.

"I'm good. A little tired still I guess," said Oliver.

"You were in the zone last night," said Jason.

"Thanks, it felt good."

"How much trimming do we have left for this session," said Jason?

"We're getting down there to the end," said Jackson. "I think one good push this morning, and we could be done till next time. Here are your eggs, Oliver. Grab some bacon too."

The trimmers, Rex and Sam, crawled out of their sleeping bag and into the kitchen for the morning breakfast. Oliver looked out the front window to the ocean. The sun was casting a warm glow over the water making it a deep earthy blue.

Friday morning now, Oliver thought. A week from now I'm going to have to be heading back to my apartment in Madison to get settled in for the school year. It seems impossibly far away from this strange place. How long can I stay here? What if Jackson doesn't give me the weed for the trip back? Do I even want to take the risk of taking all that back? For what? My asshole brother who wasn't man enough to do his own dirty work? Who offered me to the hands of fate to take his risks for him?

"Good morning everyone," said Star, coming over to the bench by the window and sitting down next to Oliver. She kissed him on the cheek and put her hand on his leg. "Good morning my brave warrior," she said in Oliver's ear.

Oliver laughed, "Why brave warrior?"

"You seemed like a brave warrior to me last night," said Star. "That's all. It felt like you were in a place where you could do anything. It was really strange, but very sexy."

Oliver smiled. It may have been the only time a woman called him sexy in his entire life. He wasn't trying to be sexy. He wasn't trying to be anything.

Charlie and Megan came out from the back together and Chewy showed up from somewhere. Mia came in the front door from outside, radiant and glowing warm from her morning yoga.

"All right everyone. Now that I've got you all here," said Jackson. "If we can get it all finished up, today will be the last day of trimming this session. As you all know, we have the annual harvest party on Horse Mountain tonight. Let's try and hit it hard this morning, so we can rest up for the party this afternoon. Bacon is over here. Anyone who wants eggs, I'm taking orders. There is toast over there, make it yourself."

"You going to trim this morning Oliver?" said Charlie.

"Yeah, I guess so. I'd like to help get finished up," said Oliver.

After breakfast all the trimmers sat down around the large table in the back of the living room. Someone put "Back To The Future" on the TV. Everyone got a pile of branches to turn into neat little buds.

Oliver's phone rang.

∞

"Mom," Oliver said, walking out the front door.

"Oliver, how is your trip?"

"It's good, Mom."

"Are you on your way home yet?"

"No, Mom. I'm still here."

"Have you heard from your brother? I've been trying to get a hold of him. It's not like him to ignore me for this long. Oliver, are you ignoring me too?"

"No, Mom. I'm talking to you right now."

"You have to get back here. You have to get back for school. School starts in a week you know. It's your senior year."

"I know that mom. I will get back when I can. I will be back in time for school."

"How is Charlie doing? Is he keeping you out of trouble? I bet his parents don't even know he's there. I bet they haven't even called him."

"Charlie is as good as ever, Mom. He met a girl."

"What? Charlie? Met a girl? No wonder why you guys are still out there. Good for him. He deserves a nice girl. I tell you Oliver, if I were your age I would have dated Charlie."

"Mom."

"What, I'm just saying. Instead of dating those bad boys, I should have dated someone sweet like Charlie."

"Charlie isn't that sweet mom."

"You don't know him like I do Oliver. I know him like a mom knows him. He is a good boy."

"Mom, that's disturbing on many levels. Anyway, how are you?"

"I'm fine, Oliver. I'm just fine. How are you, my son? Have you met any girls?"

"Not really."

"What does not really mean? Either you have or you haven't."

"Well, sort of. Yes, but. I like her, but."

"Oliver. You have met a girl. Have you slept with her?"

"Mom."

"It's important."

"It's not important to talk about it with you."

"I am your mother Oliver. You can tell me anything."

"No I can't. Can you imagine talking about your sex life with your mom?"

"That's different. My mom wasn't as open minded as I am about this sort of thing."

"It's still gross Mom. I love you and all, but for fuck sake."

"Oliver. Don't talk like that. So do you like her? What's her name?"

"Her name is Star."

"So her parents are hippies I take it."

"Well. Yes."

"My child. What are you getting into out there? Well, you are growing up. I guess I'm going to have to accept that. So are you going to date her?"

"She lives in Oregon, Mom. She goes to college in Oregon."

"So."

"Well, I live in Wisconsin. She lives in Oregon. I barely know her. Yes, I like her, but it's a big thing to just ask someone who you don't really know that well to have a long distance relationship with you. Then what? Even when we both graduate college, either she has to move to the land locked state of Wisconsin, or I have to move all the way to the West coast."

"So you'll sleep with her, but you won't ask her to date? What kind of world are we living in?"

"Mom, I didn't say I slept with her."

"Did you?"

"Well, yes."

"I knew it. I probably won't even get to meet her, will I? What if she's pregnant? Did she get tested for diseases? Obviously she is willing to open those legs up. Oliver, this isn't what I meant by figure out what life is about."

"Mom, your acting crazy. Besides, I thought you said you were open minded about this stuff?"

"Oh Oliver. I'm sorry. I've been pretty emotional these days. I just don't want to see my little boy get his heart broken."

"I'll be fine mom. I'd like to say 'I know what I'm doing' but I don't. I'm doing the best I can. I think I have learned a lot since I've been out here. I swam in the ocean. Star is a surfer. You should see her Mom. She's pretty amazing. Her whole family surfs."

"That's really good, Oliver. I'm so happy for you. Tell your brother to call me when you talk to him, will you?"

"Mom. I'm still here."

"I know you are, Oliver. I have to get going now. Tell Charlie I'm very proud of him. I'm proud of you too my son. I really am."

"Mom, you don't have to go. We can talk more if you want. I'll tell you anything."

"No. I've got to get going Oliver. I have to get up and get my day started. I have a big day today. I love you Oliver."

"I love you too, Mom. What do you have going on today? Mom?"

"Have a great day, Oliver. I'll talk to you soon. I have to go."

"Mom, I miss you."

"I miss you too. Goodbye Oliver."

∞

Oliver stared out at the ocean. Not really seeing anything. In that moment, he felt as though he were far out on the ocean in a life raft. He felt at drift.

Inside he could here laughter. A week ago, he thought to himself, he probably would have just found a blanket and went to the beach to curl up with his thoughts. I am not the same Oliver that I was a week ago, he thought. Now there are people inside, who, if they don't quite love me, at least they like me. They can laugh. They can forget about the rest of the troubles in the rest of their world, for now at least. I am here now. I know how to laugh. I can laugh too.

As he walked back in the door Star caught his gaze. He sat in a spot at the table next to her. She gently touched his leg.

"Where are Megan and Charlie?" asked Oliver.

"In the back bedroom," said Star.

"We sleep in that bed," said Oliver.

"I imaging they are probably not the only people to ever do what they are doing in there, before we slept in it Oliver."

"That's true," said Oliver.

"Oliver," said Sam. "You go to college, don't you? What is your major?"

"English," said Oliver.

"Jason, you were an English major weren't you?" said Rex.

"Yeah," said Jason. "English Lit, with a minor in Philosophy."

"Didn't you go to Stanford or something?" said Rex. "Did your parents pay for that?"

"No, I had mainly scholarships," said Jason. "My parents were pretty liberal about the whole venture. My dad never graduated high school, and he owned his own business. He didn't care if I went to college or joined the army. He just wanted me to do something that would be productive for my life. My mom thought going to school for English Lit was wasting my education on bullshit that wouldn't do me any good when I got out."

"Was it productive for your life?" said Sam. "You live pretty much off the grid now. Do you think it helped prepare you for that?"

"I think so," said Jason. "Not so much in what I learned, although many of the philosophers that I got into shaped my thinking. I think it shaped my learning process. It was a safe place to help learn how to adapt to learning in different environments. It was a time in my life when I was sort of searching for teachers. I wanted to learn and I absorbed a lot."

"Did you ever intend to use your college education to get a 'real job'?" said Sam.

"When I was in doing my undergraduate work I thought maybe I would get out and do something, or maybe come back to school and get my masters and doctorates, to become a professor myself. I did eventually go back. I do have a master's degree. I've just never been able to convince myself that plugging into the system was the best way I could contribute. After my undergrad I took a couple of good books and went on the road for close to a year. I had enough money saved up to keep a steady supply of second hand philosophy books coming in. I traveled up and down the coast and stayed in towns that had a good used book store. I slept mainly wherever I could be safely out of the rain and cold. I went up to Seattle in the heat of the summer and traveled down to southern Cali when it got cold up north."

"Was it scary," asked Oliver.

"It's hard to explain really. Yeah, there were a few scary times. For the most part though, it was pretty reasonable. Not many people bother with you when they think they know what to expect. I just looked like any other street kid. Most people just ignored me. There's actually a pretty good network out there of wayward travelers. If you know the right places to go, you can get food and shelter pretty much anywhere. Beyond that, all I really wanted anyway were some good books."

"Shit, if your parents weren't cool with you getting an English degree, what did they think of the traveling like a bum thing," said Rex.

"Yeah, they weren't crazy about it. I told them I was being educated by life. I tried to play it off like I was continuing my education on my own. They weren't very impressed. My dad thought it was time for me to get a real job and my mom thought I was going to get killed."

"How did you end up here?" said Oliver.

"I really liked Arcata," said Jason. "The used book store was great. I figured it was due to the college in town, but beyond that, the people have a pretty free mindset and I gravitated towards it."

"How did you get in with these guys," said Sam.

"I actually met Mia first. You've got to remember, I only did the living on the street thing for a couple of years before I went back to school for my MFA. After I got the masters, I moved up here and got a job at the Wildberries grocery store in Arcata. I was living in a little one bedroom college apartment trying to figure out what I was going to do next with my life. I met her in the little coffee shop down by the square. I was reading "Letters from a Stoic," by Seneca, and we struck up a conversation about Stoic philosophy."

"So that's how you ended up here?" said Oliver.

"No. It ended up that some people who I worked with at the grocery store trimmed for these guys, and they asked me if I was looking for some extra cash. I was saving up for whatever it was that I was going to do next, and I agreed. They brought me here, and now I've been trimming with them a couple of times a year for the last few years. Between this and selling mushrooms, that's the only thing I really do to make money."

"You sell mushrooms?" said Oliver. "Like the magic kind?"

"Yes, I grow Psilocybin mushrooms. Psilocybe Cyanofbrillosa is the variety I cultivate. It's indigenous to this area. I grow a little more than I need for personal, and help out friends with the rest. It's not something I do with the intent of getting rich. I only take them once or twice a year, myself, and I grow a few for people I know. That's about it. I don't live an extravagant lifestyle. By living simply I was able to save up enough money to buy the little 5 acre piece of land that I live on now. I have a little ecosystem there that provides almost all the food I need for the year. There aren't many things I actually need money for. A couple times a year I like to travel, and that takes a few bucks, not much though, I travel pretty light."

"Star said you live in a Yurt," said Oliver. "What's that like?"

"I don't know. Like anything else I guess," said Jason. "It's like most houses, but it doesn't have any corners."

"Isn't a yurt some kind of Mongolian dwelling?" said Sam.

"Yeah, they were original used by the Mongolian nomadic people in the steps of Central Asia. Genghis Kahn's people lived in them as they conquered almost the entire Asian Continent, and a good chunk of the Middle East. They're still very common in Mongolia," said Jason. "I like it because it's semi-permanent, and affordable. I'm not tied down and enslaved to a mortgage. Not only that, I can literally pick up my house and move it anytime I want. Not that I want to, but if I want to move it to another location on my property, it can be done relatively easy. Try doing that with a normal house."

"Do you have running water?" said Star.

"I have a natural spring on my property. It's above my house. I have a gravity fed water system. I don't have running water in my toilet, but it's a self-composting system. I have an outhouse."

"We had an outhouse when I was a kid for almost 5 years," said Star.

"It's not so bad," said Jason. "I live in the foothills of the mountains, and in the winter it can get a little chilly. You get used to it though."

Charlie and Megan emerged from the back of the house, freshly showered and smiling. They took their usual seats and started working. The midmorning sun was cresting towards the ocean.

"This is the last of it guys," said Chewy, carrying one last half full looking bag into the living room.

"What about you guys?" said Oliver, to Rex and Sam.

"We have been friends with Mia, Jackson and Chewy since they lived in Berkley," said Sam.

"We live in Oakland now," said Rex. "I work at a small brewery and Sam is a lawyer at a law firm that specializes in human rights."

"Holy shit," said Oliver. "I didn't know you were a lawyer."

"I'm not dressed like one now," smiled Sam.

"You must not need the money then," said Charlie.

"I work for a nonprofit, and we're not rich by any stretch of the imagination, but no we don't really need the money," said Sam. "We come up here to get away and hang out with cool people. Besides, the harvest fest party is the best party of the year. It's the only time all year we get to eat mushrooms. There's just too much going on in the city to get any benefit from them, in my opinion," said Sam.

"What do you mean benefit?" said Charlie. "Don't they just mess you up?"

"Mushrooms are a funny thing," said Jason. "They can be many things to many people. If you take them just to blow your mind, you never really know what's going to happen. It may be good—it may be not so good. You never exactly know what's going to happen. If you take them with a lot of turmoil in your mind, or a lot of anger, you are more likely to have a bad time. The mushrooms are not to be taken lightly. They will show you things. Things about yourself. Things about others. Sometimes it seems as though they have a voice of their own, completely separate from your conscious mind."

"They sound pretty dangerous," said Oliver. "Why do you take them?"

"They can be," said Jason. "You need to respect them. Once you learn them, they are a little more predictable. Knowing how much you take is very important. It's never a good policy to just start eating handfuls of them without knowing how much you're taking, or what it's going to do to you. There is this thing called 'set and setting.' It means being in a safe place with good people. It's a very important key, especially if you're a beginner. Don't take mushrooms with ass holes, unless they're taking the same amount as you. Don't take mushrooms by yourself, at least the first time, and preferably with someone who is experienced."

"What does it feel like?" said Charlie. "Do you hallucinate?"

"It depends on what you mean by hallucinate," said Jason. "I've never actually seen anything visually with my eyes open that wasn't really there. Sitting with my eyes closed on a large dose, now that's a little different. Terrence McKenna used to talk about sitting with his eyes closed on what he called a 'heroic dose' of 5 dried grams and seeing elves. I've never quite experienced that though."

"Terrence McKenna used to hang out at my house when I was a kid," said Star. "He was a friend of my parents. Well, my dad. My mom thought he was a megalomaniac. I guess she liked him, but thought he was pretty far gone."

"No way," said Jason. "I've read most of his books, and I've seen videos of him speaking in the 80's and 90's, but I never met the man. He was a little before my time. I was only a teenager when he was still giving his talks."

"I was really young when he was around. I don't remember him much. I remember he had a really funny laugh," said Star.

"So it sounds like there are a lot of warnings with taking mushrooms," said Oliver. "Are they safe?"

"Depends what you mean by safe," said Jason. "They are powerful medicine. As with any medicine proper dosage is important. It's common for people to think that they are really ready for a huge trip, and just pound a bunch of mushrooms. Usually you don't get much out of that. Often times you do get to feel like you're dying, which can be a powerful thing, and often very terrifying if you're not ready for it. No one ever actually dies from mushrooms. It's your ego that thinks its dying. If you're ever tripping and you feel like you're dying, don't panic. It's your ego. It's that thing inside you that thinks it's separate from the rest of the universe. The best thing to do at that point, the hardest thing for a beginner, is to stand over your ego and just watch it fade away."

"That's some trippy shit," said Charlie.

"It is," said Jason.

"What does it feel like? How much should you take?" said Oliver. "You're talking like this is something that should be prescribed by a doctor."

"Everyone is different," said Jason. "One dried gram will generally get you to a place where you feel pretty euphoric. If you're a sensitive person you may get some intense moments, but they will always pass if you let them. Two dried grams or so will take you a little deeper. Three dried grams and you are getting into the deep work area. Four to five dried grams and you're getting in the big dose area, it's hard to know what you're getting into at that point, it could be great, or it could bring you to your knees and make you answer for all your sins. Remember that three and a half grams is about an eighth. It's actually a fair amount of plant matter, so when you get to that point, you've eaten quite a few. Anything beyond five grams is pretty far out there, and I don't recommend it to anyone, especially someone who doesn't know what they're getting into. Most people who know what they're getting into would seldom attempt it, without proper intent. In my personal experience there's no need to go there."

"If I take them will I end up living in a yurt out in the middle of the wilderness?" said Oliver. "No offense of course."

"None taken," laughed Jason. "Mushrooms aren't the reason I live in a yurt. Well, maybe a little, but I was a traveler and felt like a nomad before I ever took mushrooms. If everyone who ever took mushrooms decided to break free from their cultural chains, we would have a lot more people in the woods than we do now I assure you. Most of the time, for me anyway, it makes me see all the delusions around me for what they are. That perspective is different for everyone. I would be in the woods with or without the mushroom. Just like someone who takes them on the weekend and goes back to their 9 to 5 job the following Monday, is probably meant to go back and reintegrate into society. That's their thing. Although, I would recommend at least one day after the trip to let your mind equilibrate."

"Looks like this is the last of it," said Rex, grabbing the last of the buds from the pile.

"Alright everyone," said Jackson, walking in from the kitchen. "Time to do a final weigh in, and then I'll square up with everyone."

24

"That's not what I meant," said Charlie

"What else does, 'yeah I would fuck another chick mean?'" said Megan.

"You asked me if I would ever get into an orgy."

"Well, I guess I know the answer," said Megan.

"I thought you meant you wanted us to try an orgy," said Charlie. "I thought it was a question. You said it like a question?"

"I didn't expect you to be so enthusiastic about it," said Megan. "Besides, if I did, it wouldn't just be so you could 'fuck a chick.'"

"What, you want me to fuck a dude," said Charlie.

"No. No, I don't want you to fuck a dude. I just wanted to know if you would ever go to a sex party. That's all," said Megan.

"I don't know?" said Charlie. "Have you ever been to a sex party?"

"Yeah, a few," said Megan.

"A few... What's a few?" said Charlie. "So like a few three? A few four?"

"I don't know? Fifteen to twenty five," said Megan.

"First of all, that's a pretty large spread. Second of all who guesses by fives? Third, how many dudes have you been with?" said Charlie.

"I'm twenty three, Charlie. I've had some time," said Megan.

"If you were to guess," said Charlie. "Would it be thirty three to eighty seven?"

"Stop, now you're just being a dick," said Megan.

"How many do you think?"

"It's not important," said Megan. "Can we just pretend I didn't even say anything about the sex party thing? I was joking anyway."

"You can't just leave it there. It's like telling someone a joke, without telling them the punch line," said Charlie.

"I don't want you to be weirded out or anything. Can we just drop it Charlie."

"Seriously? You don't want me to be weirded out? Now I'm super weirded out. Is it like two hundred and fifty?"

"No, I have not slept with two hundred and fifty men. I haven't even slept with that many people total."

"What, total? What the fuck?" said Charlie.

"Fine. I'll tell you. But you have to promise not to get mad," said Megan.

"I promise," said Charlie. "It's just a number.

"I've slept with ninety four guys, and forty three women," said Megan.

"Okay. Yeah, so it's just a number. That's like what? That's like one hundred and thirty seven, right? That's like an exact number. Wow... wow."

"You sound mad," said Megan.

"Oh, you know. It's not every day that the girl you are falling in love with tells you she slept with one hundred and thirty seven other people. I'm not mad. I'm something, but I'm not sure mad is the thing that I am."

"You're falling in love with me?" said Megan.

"I thought I was?" said Charlie.

"Oh and now you're not? I'm honest with you. I share my secrets. And now you're not in love with me anymore?"

"It's just... You know. A lot to take in. All at once."

"Charlie, it's not like you're a virgin or anything. How many people have you slept with?"

"Never mind. Just never mind. I don't really want to talk about this anymore," said Charlie.

"You can't never mind me now. I just told you my biggest secret."

"Your biggest secret. Your biggest secret. One hundred and forty other people know your biggest secret."

"It's not actually that many. Are you a...virgin, Charlie?"

"Not really. No. You're my second. I slept with a girl at a party one time on a dare. There, sue me. You're the only one who's ever slept with me for me, and now I find out you would have slept with anyone. Fuck. Fuck this."

"Oh Charlie. Oh, no Charlie. I'm so sorry."

"Whatever. I knew it was too good to be true."

"It is true. I didn't lie to you. This has been great."

"I wanted more. I wanted more than great. I wanted a relationship for once in my life. Great is stupid. I wanted real."

"Charlie, you live in Wisconsin, I live in Oregon. How would it work?"

"I hate Wisconsin. I have nothing in Wisconsin. I could move. I could move to Oregon. We could be together."

"Oh Charlie. I really like you. I really do. I just don't know if that would work. We barely know each other. How long has it been? Like five days?"

"It's been long enough. I think I love you. I didn't want it to go down like this. I wanted it to be special. I wanted us to sit on the beach and I would tell you I love you and you would tell me I love me back."

"I would tell you I love me?"

"You know what I mean," said Charlie. It's like we're having a fight. I just wanted it to be special, that's all. And this isn't."

"Charlie, I would love to sit on the beach with you. Here. I would love to watch the sun go down with you again, here in California. Charlie, we are here. That is where this thing we have is. Can we just be that? Can we just be what we are here and not worry about what we will be when we leave this place? I've had a great time with you, Charlie. You're a great guy and I know you can find someone better than me. You're smart, and funny and good in bed. I can't believe you were practically a virgin."

"Beginners luck I guess."

"See, you're funny. Come here. Kiss me Charlie."

"No, I... I can't."

"Shhh... Just come over here," said Megan. "We're still here."

25

"I'm going to miss that silly hat," said Star, as they walked down the beach.

"Me too," said Oliver. "I don't even notice it anymore."

"If you pull it down far enough you can barely see your black eye," Star smiled.

"I think the embarrassment will linger long after the black eye," said Oliver.

"You shouldn't be embarrassed, he's an asshole. He sucker punched you. Besides, you got the girl right."

"I guess you're right," said Oliver. "So have you ever been to one of these parties at Horse Mountain?"

"Yeah, I've been the last two years in a row. It's my favorite gathering of the year."

"What's it like?" said Oliver.

"Well, you're going to have to find out I guess," said Star. "Every gathering is a little different. The only rules are no headlights after dark. If you show up in a car after dark, you have to park your car down the hill and walk up. It's kind of like an unspoken rule that you're supposed to know. It's dark, but your eyes adjust."

"So there is no light? No fires or anything?"

"Well, most people have a little flashlight or something for emergencies. And almost everyone has a glow stick, but they don't put off much light, and they don't dull the sky. I think the idea is to get a good view of the night sky. It's a pretty amazing view," said Star.

"Look, there's the trail back up to the house. We should head in. I bet they're starting to get ready to go."

Oliver looked over his shoulder as they climbed the steep bank up to the house. The ocean air fanned over his face. The afternoon waves rolled into the shore. He found himself starting to miss it already.

"Okay everybody," said Jackson, as they entered the house. "Here's a box of glow sticks, take as many as you think you're gonna need. If you don't already have a flashlight, take one of these small ones for emergencies. If everyone's ready, we're going to head up to the mountain in a few minutes. How many of us are there? Wait, Oliver where's Charlie?"

"I don't know, we just got back," said Oliver.

"Probably somewhere with Megan," said Star.

"Make sure they know the game plan. We're leaving in a few minutes. How many do we have?"

"Including the wayward lovers we have ten with us," said Mia.

"Who wants to drive," said Jackson. "I'll be taking my car. Oliver, I'm not going to tell you to drive, but it would be great if we could take your van. We could fit everyone in two vehicles that way."

"Yeah, that's no problem," said Oliver.

"Everyone grab sleeping bags. Mia packed a cooler full of food, and we have enough water to hydrate a herd of elephants. Oliver, if you're not feeling up to driving by the time everyone else starts to leave in the morning, we can just stay longer."

"Do we need tents or something?" said Oliver.

"If you were in a tent you couldn't see the view," said Mia, smiling. "A pillow a sleeping bag and a sweat shirt, if you have one, should be fine. There is no rain in the forecast."

26

They headed south down the Highway 101, past McKinleyville and inland on Highway 299 just before Arcata. The drive seemed as though it were taking a long time. Oliver thought about it, and then thought if this drive seems long, how long will the drive home be? After passing Blue Lake the road got more hilly and winding.

"How far out here is it?" asked Oliver.

"Just far enough," said Chewy who was sitting in the passenger seat. "It's far enough out that no one will bother coming out here without a good reason."

"How many people do you think are going to be there?" said Oliver.

"It's hard to say," said Chewy. "Probably a couple hundred."

"Wow that seems like a lot."

"Yeah, maybe? If you need anything, find Mia or myself."

"Isn't it going to be dark up there? How will I find you?"

"It's not that big of an area. You'll find us if you really need us," said Chewy.

"Why would I need you?"

"You may not," said Chewy.

They turned off the 299 onto a smaller highway, then to another back road. They were climbing in elevation.

"This is Horse Mountain," said Chewy.

They turned onto a small road that wound up the mountain. A car that Oliver had not seen before sped up behind him and followed.

They twisted and turned up the little mountain road. Up up around, around and up again. Finally reaching a narrow gravel road and they followed Jackson in the Subaru up it.

They pulled in behind a small row of cars. The car behind them pulled in too. As they were getting out of their car and stretching, another car pulled behind the row.

Everyone piled out of the cars. They could hear a couple of bongos from the top of the hill. It wasn't a steady rhythm like the night before. It sounded more like a warm up from a band. A few beats, then stop. A few more from a different area, then stop.

Jackson and Rex grabbed the cooler out of the back of Jackson's car and carried it up the hill. Everyone grabbed their sleeping bags and headed up. They were about 25 parked cars from the top.

At the very top were a series of big towers. Oliver thought they looked like they could be used to communicate with aliens. They looked strangely out of place in this setting, but why else would someone build a road all the way up to the top here?

They found a spot near another group that Jackson and Mia seemed to know. Several people lit joints and started passing them around. Blankets were spread on the ground.

"Alright guys," said Jason, to Oliver, Charlie, Star and Megan, as they sat in a little circle. "These are mushroom chocolates. Each one has 1 gram of dried mushrooms in it. I put them in chocolate for stuff like this because some people don't like the taste of the mushrooms. The chocolate just makes it easier. None of you are on anti-depressants are you? Good, that shit doesn't mix well. Since this is the first time for Oliver and Charlie, I recommend no more than one or two, but I'm going to leave it up to you. I'm going to let your ego decide."

"I'll take one," said Star.

"Me too," said Megan.

"How about you Oliver?" said Jason.

"I don't really know. I've never done them before. I'm not sure."

"You don't have to take any," said Jason. "I'm sure you will have a great time no matter what. No one needs to take mushrooms."

"I'll take four," said Charlie.

"Four is a pretty powerful dose Charlie," said Jason. "How about we start off a little slower. I think two will treat you pretty well."

"I'll take three," said Charlie.

"Okay," said Jason. "Here you go."

"I'll take two," said Oliver.

The chocolates were in the shape of bunny rabbits, like the mold had come from an Easter candy making set. Oliver took his two chocolates and bit into one. It tasted kind of chalky. Jason reached into the cooler, grabbed a couple of waters, and tossed one to each of them.

Charlie had already powered through all three chocolates as Oliver slowly nibbled at his, starting with the ears.

"Hey look, there's my mom and dad," said Star, getting up and running to meet them as they crested the hill.

"Holy shit," said Charlie. "Is it fucked up that Star's mom and dad are here?"

"They're in the same business as Jackson," said Oliver. "It's not that weird. Besides, I don't think that it's their first time at a gathering like this."

"Howdy folks," Star's dad said walking over.

"Wild Bill," said Jackson.

"Hello Melissa," said Mia, standing up to give them both hugs.

"How's everything going?" said Bill.

"We're just getting settled in," said Jackson.

"Looks like there are going to be a decent amount of people this year," said Bill.

"Yeah, it's starting to happen," said Jackson. "You guys need anything?"

"Oliver," said Charlie. "I need to talk to you. Can we go for a walk?"

"Of course," said Oliver, standing up and stretching his legs.

The view was amazing. Rolling hills and an ocean of trees as far as the eye could see. The sun was setting in the west and now about an inch over the horizon. Oliver couldn't see the ocean but he thought he could tell where the big blank spot was to the west where the ocean would be.

Oliver and Charlie walked towards the western point of the mountain, just away from the main part of the group. People seemed to keep coming in over the little crest of the hill by the road.

"How many people do you think there are?" asked Oliver.

"I don't know? Maybe a hundred?" said Charlie.

"Do you feel anything yet?" said Oliver.

"I don't know? I feel high still? I don't know what mushrooms are supposed to feel like," said Charlie.

"I think I feel something," said Oliver. "The colors seem more colorful."

"Hey Oliver, I got kind of a problem," said Charlie.

"What's up Charlie?"

"It's Megan. She's been with like 140 people."

"What?" laughed Oliver. "Including you?"

"Good question? I don't think I asked her if I was included. And don't fucking laugh man. I'm serious. She has been with like 137 people. She knew the exact number. Guys and girls," said Charlie.

"I'm sorry Charlie. I'm not trying to make fun of you. It just sounded funny that's all."

"I'm in love with her Oliver. How could it work though? Does she feel the same way, or am I just another one of her numbers? I mentioned moving out here, out to Oregon, and she pretty much laughed at me. I don't think she's serious about it at all."

"Don't take it too hard, Charlie. Everyone has a first love. You can't just marry the first girl you sleep with."

"It's just that, she's so cool. She's so fun. I just want to be with her. I love her, Oliver."

"I know you do Charlie. Don't be so hard on yourself, brother. We have to go home soon anyway."

"Home," said Charlie. "Home seems so far away. What is it, like a couple thousand miles? It might as well be a million."

"It does seem like a long way and a long time ago," said Oliver.

"I think I'm feeling something now," said Charlie.

"Hey, instead of sitting here missing Megan, you should go spend some time with her, before our time here is over," said Oliver.

"You think she even wants to hang out with me?" said Charlie.

"You two looked pretty close in the car on the ride over," said Oliver. "Don't think too much about the leaving part right now. It hasn't happened yet."

"You going to come back over with me?" said Charlie.

"No, I'm gonna to sit here for a while and watch the sun go down. I'll be over in a little bit."

Oliver sat and looked out to the horizon. The pine trees in the distance seemed to glow an amazing green. The sky was dark blue, and moved to light blue and yellow orange near the tops of the trees. The sun seemed as though it was gently crashing down towards the horizon. The trees got darker and darker as it fell.

The drums were still sporadic in the background. The night air was getting cool and Oliver was glad he had brought a sweat shirt. How many sunsets had he seen now?

Faster and faster the sun slipped down...a second later...SPLOOSH...the last ray shot out and hit Oliver directly between the eyes, nearly knocking him backwards before smoothly slipping beneath the trees and extinguishing itself in the unseen distant ocean. The drums began to beat in the background. Boom batta boom batta boom boom boom...

It wasn't quite dark yet, but Oliver could already see the stars above him starting to poke though the lightness.

"It's going to be a beautiful night," said Mia.

"I can already see the stars," said Oliver. It was getting darker, but he could still see very clearly. Mia sat down beside him. She was radiant. Her skin seemed to shimmer in the dim light. Her edges were perfectly symmetrical.

"How has your trip to California been so far?" said Mia.

"It's been amazing," said Oliver. "I've never experienced anything like it. I feel like I owe you guys a lot."

"Owe is too big of a word to place on your experience here. You don't owe us anything, Oliver. It has been a blessing to have you and Charlie stay with us."

"I love you," said Oliver. "I am in love with you. You are the most amazing person. The most amazing human being I have ever met."

"I love you too, Oliver. And I thank you. There are a lot of emotions coming through you right now."

"For real. I fell in love with you the first time I saw you. And not just because you were naked from the waist up."

"Love is a powerful thing. It is beautiful. It takes many shapes in your mind. It takes many forms. You have been having this experience since the moment you stepped on our doorstep. This moment is a continuation of that moment. In your eyes, I stepped into the room and saved you. Now we are here."

"No, it's not just that you saved me. Or I think that you saved me. It's how you are. How you talk."

"I try to only speak the truth as I see it."

"See that's it. You don't bullshit. You don't try and impress anyone. You are authentic. You are the truth."

"Thank you, Oliver. You are a truth seeker too. Follow the truth, and you will be on the right path."

"I'm sorry if I'm being weird. I'm not trying to be with you or anything. I know you're in a relationship. Shit, I practically am. Or I might be. Whatever. I just feel like I have to tell you how much I appreciate you."

"I appreciate you too, Oliver. I am not the truth. I try to let the truth come through me. You can do the same. Anyone can. For some it's easier than others. It depends on how they have been conditioned. I see it just on the surface for you Oliver."

"Half the time I don't know what the truth is," said Oliver.

"Yes you do. It's always there."

"I think that most of us are trying to hide the truth," said Oliver. "Like we have this shell over ourselves, protecting our inside thoughts with our outside shell that is like a shield. We can act tough or act shy, but it's all an act. It's like we are pretending to be who we are in front of other people. I do it all the time. I felt like I loved you from the moment I saw you, and I spent all week trying to act like I didn't have these feelings."

"Sometimes we feel like we have to hide ourselves. I think it's the force within us that psychologists like to call our 'ego,' trying to protect the idea of who we think we are. When we hide or when we lie, we are trying to protect the personal myth that we carry of ourselves. As individuals we protect that idea of who we are, based on the idea of who we think we are or who we want to become. Sometimes we are dishonest with others and sometimes, more often than we know, we are dishonest with ourselves."

"What is the ego?" said Oliver. "Why do we even need it?"

The ego, in a way, is the self-fulfilling prophecy that our personal myth manifests, in any given moment, to help define who we are to ourselves. It is the thing that makes us an individual and unique onto ourselves. It does have a functioning purpose. In practical terms, it helps us to separate our inner self from the outside world in the same way our physical body creates boarders around who we are in physical space.

"That is very deep," said Oliver.

"It is," said Mia, "but we don't have go to that level to understand most of our personal truth issues."

"Why is the truth so hard for us to see?" said Oliver.

"The truth is the most present in the moment. By the time we put thoughts to it, it is open to interpretation. Your perception of the truth will follow the path your thoughts have been trained towards, because that is the lens with which you have been conditioned to see the truth."

"What do you mean?" said Oliver. "Who conditions us?"

"Our interpretation of the truth is malleable. It is easy to manipulate. We are very easy to fool, even by our own thoughts. We are conditioned to see the truth through the lens of our environment. There are many shaping factors in our life, our parents, our culture, church, state, all things in which we are born into. Most of the time it isn't intentional deception. Our parents, generally speaking, just want the best for us. They shape our vision based on what they have learned. They want us to understand the truth as they have come to know it, because that's what feels safe. People, even very good people, are not easily swayed from their idea of the truth. Many paths are well-worn by the feet that have walked them before. It is easier to follow a well-worn path, because it takes the least amount of effort. It feels less dangerous and is easier on the feet."

"Is that how people are brain washed?"

"Yes. Sometimes it is intentional. Sometimes we are forced into understanding someone else's perspective because the alternative is a severe negative consequence. Such is the case for many dictatorships that have power concentrated in the hands of few and need to use force, or the perception of it, to control many. Very strong and intelligent people can be trained to understand things in ways that don't make any literal sense. If you can control someone's mind, you don't have to use physical pressure to keep them in the path that has been created for them to follow."

"Like our war on drugs?" said Oliver. "When I go home, if I get caught with all the plants that my brother is paying many thousands of dollars for, I will be put in jail because our country has determined that having these plants warrants a negative consequence. I know that the threat of force is supposed to keep me from doing what the government doesn't want me to do."

"Yes," said Mia.

"I don't really want to think about that right now. I can't think about that right now."

"Okay, Oliver," said Mia. "Just understand that you are manipulating your own perception of the truth."

"I just want to know why it's so hard to deal with the truth. Why can't we just tell each other how we feel?" said Oliver.

"It takes a lot of strength and courage to say exactly what we think all the time. I think of Jackson. He is very strong. He always says exactly what he sees. Unfortunately, he often uses it as a weapon, like he's in a battle. He will say things to get the other person to respond, so he can go on the attack and control the situation."

"Does that bother you?" said Oliver.

"No. He can't, or chooses not to do it to me. I can see it coming. I know him too well. Besides, one of the greatest gifts to give someone in this life is the gift of forgiveness," smiled Mia.

"That's a really hard one for me," said Oliver. "I get angry and stay angry at people. I have a hard time letting things go. I'm so angry at my brother right now. Even though this experience is amazing, I have a hard time forgiving."

"Forgiveness is as easy as letting go. It takes a lot of energy to hold onto anger. If you don't forgive someone, every time you see or think of them you have a negative response. It can almost feel physical at times, like a pit in your stomach. Then you have to keep reminding yourself of it. You can think through all the different ways this person has done you wrong. You can feel every blow and imagine how they might hurt you in the future. It's like they continue to hurt you without even being there. You are hurting yourself just thinking about it. It's much better to just let it go. Forgiveness is freedom."

"What if they are continuing to hurt you? What if they are oppressing you? What if they are abusing you?"

"I was abused as a child. When you are in it, it is very hard. It is hard to see that person as anything but a monster. It's hard if you're physically trapped in a situation. When you're trapped, the best freedom is away from the person who is hurting you. Forgiveness is easiest when you have no need for the alarm that you are feeling. It's when you are sitting alone, or feeling like you have to protect yourself from others, that forgiveness has the most benefit."

"I don't know if I should forgive my brother. He should be here, not me. But if he were here, I wouldn't be."

"You can always forgive," said Mia. "Look at the sky."

"It's beautiful," said Oliver. "I don't know if I've ever seen this many stars all at once."

"There is no light pollution up here. You know...the night sky doesn't always tell the whole truth. When we look at it, we see only what we can see. We see a bunch of stars. The truth is that many of them have been burnt out for thousands of years, and all we are seeing is the light that they are still sending our direction. The sky is not lying to us. It just is how the sky is. Things are not always exactly as they look."

"That sky is just so vast," said Oliver. "It's hard to even imagine how big it is. It's hard to even understand."

"And it's similar to the same night sky our ancestors have been looking at for all of the many thousands of years humans have been on this planet. Imagine how many people have looked up in wonder at the night sky," said Mia.

"Probably all of them," said Oliver.

"You don't have to try to understand everything," said Mia. "Things will happen as they happen no matter how much you understand, or don't understand."

"Hey, Oliver, is that you," said Star coming up behind them.

"Yeah, over here," said Oliver.

"We've been looking for you guys. Charlie is really looking for you."

"Coming," said Oliver.

They walked back over towards the hill top. It seemed as though there were twice as many people as when Oliver had gone off the edge of the mountain to sit. He found Charlie sitting on his sleeping bag drinking water.

"Oliver, there you are my friend. Where have you been?" said Charlie.

"Sitting in the same spot you left me at a while ago," said Oliver.

"I couldn't find you. I wanted to talk to you," said Charlie. "Something is really happening. I feel everything all at once. I feel the whole world. It's all so fucking real right now. I'm dying Oliver."

"We're all dying," said Jackson, who was sitting on the cooler.

"I don't think you're helping, Jackson," said Oliver. "Charlie, you're not dying."

"We die a little every day we live," said Jackson. "But unless you fall off a cliff, you probably won't die tonight, son."

"Oh shit, I could fall off a cliff?" said Charlie. "I need to stay away from the edge."

"How much did you eat?" said Jackson.

"Three of those chocolates," said Charlie.

"It's your first time isn't it," said Jackson.

"Yeah," said Oliver.

"Who fucking told you it would be a good idea to take that much on your first time out? Whatever, doesn't matter. It's best just to let shit go by," said Jackson. "You are not dying. It's your ego. Your 'self' is being over ridden. You are passing beyond the ego that usually runs things in your day to day life."

"But I like being myself," said Charlie. "I don't want to lose myself."

"Don't worry it will come back. Maybe a little different self, but everything will come back. It's like hitting a reset button."

"But, but I don't want to change," said Charlie.

"The best thing to do is tell your ego to fuck off. Stand over it and watch it die. You don't need it," said Jackson.

"Then why do we have it?" said Charlie.

"I don't know," said Jackson. "Product of evolution, I guess. It's a fiction we tell ourselves about who we think we are."

"What is it?" said Charlie. "How do we know it's even there?"

"Have you ever walked into a room and looked at a glass of water sitting on a table, and said to yourself, 'there is a glass of water. I think I'll have a drink.' That's your ego talking. That voice inside your own head. The narrative that you create about the world. The glass of water would be there even if you didn't talk to yourself about it. You would still be thirsty and still take a drink even if you didn't have this running commentary in your head. Your ego only knows English because your ego only knows the things that you know, or that you think you know."

"That's fucked up," said Charlie. "Holy shit, that's fucked up. Who in the fuck am I?"

"You guys should go for a walk," said Jackson. "Think about what's happening around you instead of what's going on inside your head for a while. If you get lost, just follow the beat of the drums. They will guide you back to the center."

"What if we fall off a cliff?" said Charlie.

"It's a round topped mountain, for the most part. There aren't many sharp drop offs around here. Just stay relatively close, don't wander downhill very far and you'll be fine."

It looked like a sea of glow light fish on top of a large fish bowl. The drums beat a steady rhythm. Many people sat in little circles talking and laughing. Many people walked around and mingled. The sun was completely gone. It was dark, but their eyes had adjusted surprisingly well.

"Charlie, are you crying?" said Oliver.

"I don't want to die, Oliver."

"You're not going to die, Charlie. You're tripping. Mornings going to come and you're going to be just fine."

"Okay, okay... I'll try to believe you. This is like the most real thing I've ever experienced."

"Hey look at this," said Oliver.

Ahead, were two people with big candles, a man and a woman. There was a large circle forming around them. They faced off and began what seemed like a rehearsed dance. They both put something in the candles and it lit up. It looked like a flaming marshmallow at the end of a chain.

They started spinning them. Their candles sat in the center. At first they walked around the edges of the circle spinning the fire. Not getting close to anyone, but making it clear what they wanted the boundaries of the circle to be. The people obliged, giving them a large clear flat circle, with the candles flickering in the center.

The man stood at one side of the large circle and the woman stood at the other. They moved to the beat of the drums, but they also seemed to move to the rhythm of each other.

They both spun two chains. They made little circles and big circles and spun the chains in different directions at the same time. The lines of the fire seemed to streak the air, and it looked like circles of constant flame.

They moved closer together and met in the middle by the candle. Their flames were getting weak. They tilted their heads back, lifted the balls of fire as high as they could reach, and extinguished them in their mouths. First one flaming ball, and then the other. They walked to the edge and dipped the balls in large cans on the edge of the circle, and walked back to the center.

They lit up on the candles and started to spin. This time they came close together. They were each spinning both of their flames in the same direction. They got so close to each other with each spin that the man's flaming circles entered the woman's flaming circles. If the timing were to become off the flames would collide.

He knelt down and tilted his head back. His arms outstretched and the flames still spinning. Each flame licking the ground as it passed. She stood over him, bringing her arms together and spinning her flames close to one another, the middle fingers she was spinning them from almost touching. She spun her circles in countering directions and with each circle the flames came so close to her face that it looked like she could put them out with her tongue. She stood over him as he lay back and the dancing flames licked his bare chest.

The drums that, before, were scattered around the mountain top, began to move in and surround the circle. A dozen or so more large candles were lit around the edge of the circle. The crowd around the circle was still growing.

The two in the center of the ring stood, bowed to the crowd and extinguished their remaining flames.

Through the crowd came a man on stilts juggling four flaming sticks. He lumbered to the center of the circle and stood juggling for a moment. One by one he caught all of the sticks in one hand, and raising them in front of his face he blew something from his mouth. A flame shot straight out from the sticks about 6 feet. With his free hand he grabbed a bottle from his back pocket, poured it into his mouth, spun 180 degrees the other direction on one stilt and blew a large orange, yellow and blue flame 6 feet in the opposite direction. He put the bottle back into his pocket and began to juggle again as he walked from the circle.

Two women appeared in the circle, both with what seemed to be batons. They dipped them into cans at opposite edges of the circle and lit them each on candles. They began dancing and leaping towards each other, spinning the flames as they circled one another.

"They're amazing, aren't they," said Star as she slid up next to Oliver.

"Unbelievable," said Oliver.

"This is really happening, isn't it," said Charlie.

"This is definitely happening," said Megan. "How are you doing, Charlie? Jackson said you were tripping out a little bit."

"I don't know yet," said Charlie. "I'm not afraid anymore. I'm not afraid of anything right now."

"Come with me," said Megan. She grabbed his arm and they walked off into the darkness.

Oliver put his arm around Star's back and she reached both arms around him and squeezed him tight.

"This all seems so real," said Oliver. "I know it's real, but there's a different quality to it. I can feel everything."

"Do you want to go sit and look at the stars," said Star.

"Yeah, where can we go?" said Oliver.

"Follow me," said Star, as she grabbed his hand and led him around the outside of the crowd.

As they passed people Oliver felt as though he could feel their moods. He could feel when someone was happy, he could see a drummer who was really intense, he saw a man standing in the back of the crowd drinking a glass of something, and he could tell he was drunk, he had a kind of closed off sense of being. Maybe he could always see things like this, Oliver thought, maybe he just never really noticed before.

They walked back to their group's coolers and each of them grabbed a water. They grabbed Oliver's sleeping bag. Chewy was alone on a sleeping mat, sitting in the lotus position. It was dark, but Oliver could tell his eyes were closed. He also sensed that they should let him be. They grabbed what they needed and walked off, making as little noise as possible.

They found a spot on the side of the hill and spread out their blanket. They sat down next to each other holding hands. He kissed her. When their lips touched he could feel her warmth. It felt like little electrical sparks tingling his mouth.

"Is this our last night together," he asked.

"I don't know," she said. "We have to get back to Oregon. We're planning on leaving tomorrow evening. So I think so."

"I feel like it's all so much bigger than me," said Oliver. "This whole thing. Look at those stars up there. So many of them, thousands, millions, billions and these are only the ones we can see. Then there is you, and there is me, sitting here on this blanket. On the top of a mountain. The two of us among all those stars and all these people. The two of us right now. Tomorrow it will be different for us. All the stars we see there will be the same, but we will be different."

"We are always different," said Star. "Everything we do makes us different in some way. I was never the same after I found out Santa Claus wasn't real. I felt like part of what I knew to be the truth wasn't real anymore."

"I don't see your parents as being the Santa Claus type," said Oliver.

"My dad said it was my mom's idea," smiled Star. "I think she was right. It's like a rite of passage for an American kid, I guess."

"I don't think I ever really believed it," said Oliver. "Maybe I should have?"

"We are here right now," said Star.

Oliver took his hat off and placed it on top of a rock. They slid into the sleeping bag and made love. It was only the two of them. On top of the mountain. Deep in the stars. Directly in the center of all the stars they could see and all the stars hidden from view. A tiny sliver of light in the center of the universe.

In those moments, maybe hours, Oliver understood every possible meaning of passion and conception, life and time, love and loss.

When they finished, they just laid there for a while. Feeling the others body against their warm skin, contrasted by the cool breeze now blowing softly past their faces.

The drums still beat in the background. There was clapping and laughing and talking. The mountain top was alive.

"Do you want to go look around?" said Star.

"Yeah," said Oliver. "I want to experience it all."

The air felt cooler now, as they slipped from the sleeping bag to their clothes. They found their groups area, took one more water to share, and headed back towards the drum circle.

In the distance, outside of the circle, they saw two people skipping and dancing along, naked. It was Megan and Charlie. They were laughing like children.

"I don't think Charlie is worried that he's going to die anymore," said Oliver.

"Or he realized that he is going to die and knows that it's okay," smiled Star.

The drum circle was still a circle, but no one was inside. The candles still rimmed the perimeter. The drums still beat, but there didn't seem to be as many.

People mingled and talked, some danced.

"What time do you think it is?" said Oliver.

"I don't know, I didn't bring my cell phone," said Star. "I would guess, about three A.M."

"Do people ever sleep here?"

"Some do. Most try and stay up to watch the sun come up on the east side of the mountain. Hey, Mom and Dad."

"Hey kids," said Wild Bill.

"Hello Star and Oliver," said Melissa. "How is your evening progressing?"

"Really well," said Star. "It is a beautiful night."

"And you, Oliver?" said Melissa.

"Oh, it's going good. Different, but good," said Oliver. "I didn't expect it to be like this."

"You ate mushrooms then," said Melissa.

Suddenly Oliver felt a little self-conscious about the fact that he had eaten mushrooms, or at least that he had told an adult about it.

"Yeah, we all ate some," said Star.

"Was it your first time?" said Wild Bill, to Oliver.

"Yes sir," said Oliver. "It was my first time trying mushrooms."

"What do you think?" said Wild Bill.

"I don't know yet?" said Oliver. "I think I'm still working on that. The thing is still kind of happening. I still feel it a little, but it's fading, I think."

"My first time was amazing," said Melissa. "Do you remember William? We were down on Big Sur. We had a huge bonfire on the beach. I thought I was in heaven. Maybe I was."

"Megan and Charlie seem to be having a good time," smiled Bill.

"They are free," said Melissa. "They look happy. Oliver, did you realize what you came here to find?"

"What do you mean? I didn't even know I was coming here," said Oliver. I didn't even really know I was going to eat mushrooms until we got up here."

"Did you find what you were looking for?" said Melissa.

"I don't really know. I guess all I'm really looking for is the truth. Right now I feel like the truth is bigger than I realized before. I feel like everything is, as it always has been, and that's okay. I don't need to know everything. I can't know everything. I can only know the truth as it comes in at any given moment. Maybe that's the drugs talking, I'm not sure? Will I still feel like this when I get back to normal? Is this real?"

"Experience is experience," said Bill. "The truth about your experience may not be important. Belief in your experience may not be necessary. The important part is how you integrate the lessons from your experience into your day-to-day life.

"It's the value judgment that you place on it that makes it real or not. I think that if you felt it, you can analyze it, no matter how you came upon those feelings. It's not always good feelings that you have when you take the plant medicines, but it is always more honest with you than you are with yourself. Sometimes it takes months or years to come to an understanding about what you have experienced."

"Did you guys eat mushrooms tonight?" asked Oliver.

"Yes," said Melissa.

27

"The sun comes up in the east and goes down in the west. The west coast is famous for its sunsets and the east coast is famous for its sunrises. When you're on the top of a mountain you get to experience it from both directions," said Star.

It was hard to tell for sure, but it seemed like about 150 people were gathered there on the eastern side of the hilltop. Spread blankets huddled close together in the before day break air. People spoke in soft hushed tones. In the distance behind them, two, sometimes three or four, drums kept a steady, yet gentle, beat.

The sky, not yet light, was getting brighter by the second. The stars had faded into the background of the light blue ceiling overhead. To the east was a jagged horizon of mountain tops. A yellow then orange line began to form over the distant range. Pinks and blues radiated from the top of the aura and began to bounce off the few small wisps of clouds.

If you looked really hard you could see by the gathering concentration of luminescence the general area where the sun was going to poke out of the distance. Slowly, slowly, slowly the sky began to brighten. The anticipation quickened the drums. The buzz of talking seemed to brighten and joy and laughter was speckled through the crowd.

"This is why I'm here. I am meant to be right here. Right now. This is it," said Oliver.

Closer, closer, closer the earth spun and the light gathered directly in the center of the distance. For a moment, everything before the horizon became dark. In an instant, a sliver of light splintered from between two cracks of peak in the distance. The drums fell silent. Not a whisper was heard.

Once it broke free it seemed to rise with astonishing speed. First a sliver, then a quarter and a half, three quarters and in the span of what seemed like two minutes the entire sun was visible above the eastern horizon. People began whistling and shouting with joy. Hooting and howling at the new day. Oliver screamed a blood curdling scream. Charlie barked and howled and whistled with two fingers at the new day sun.

28

The drive back to Patrick's Point seemed almost as a blur, it flowed as easily as the sun setting and rising. Everyone had packed up and got back in their vehicles almost wordlessly. The sky became blue and sun drenched as the road wound down to the little house on the coast.

"Everything will be ready for you tomorrow morning, Oliver," said Jackson, as he disappeared down the dim hallway to his bedroom.

Oliver, Charlie, Star and Megan all made their way back to the little bedroom, and for one last time, all four crawled into the bed and fell asleep.

28.5

"Oliver, Oliver I have to leave," whispered Star.

"What... what time is it," said Oliver.

"It's about 4 o'clock," said Star. "Megan and I are going to head back to Oregon."

"Can you stay for one more day? I think we're leaving tomorrow. I think that's what Jackson meant when he said everything will be ready for me tomorrow," said Oliver propping himself up on his elbows, and looking around. Megan and Charlie had already gotten up and were somewhere other than the bed they had all fallen asleep in.

"We need to go. We have to move into our new house for the school year. We have to have all our stuff out of the apartment we are in now by Monday. If we leave now, we will have all day tomorrow to move."

"It just seems so sudden," said Oliver. "All of this. Like all of the sudden it's just over."

"We can't stop time. Maybe next year we can do it again," said Star. "Same time, same place."

"Yeah," said Oliver. "Next time."

He walked her out of the bedroom and down the hall into the sweet dank smell of the living room. The light danced through the cracks in the vertical blinds. The somber air was sweet with the smell of fresh smoke.

Some of the trimmers had already left. Star had already packed her things into the car. Megan and Charlie were standing by the car, embracing and talking and laughing quietly.

"Thank you," said Oliver.

"It was a great week. Your black eye's going away, a little bit," she said slipping into the driver's seat of her car. "I will miss your black eye. It's kind of sexy."

Megan fell into the passenger seat and they waved and blew kisses as they drove away.

Rex and Sam had already gone. Jason was in the process of packing up his bed roll as Oliver and Charlie walked back into the house.

"Does this all seem too weird," said Oliver.

"The coolest girl I've ever met is gone. She's just gone," said Charlie.

"It's your first broken heart," said Oliver. "There are lots of girls out there. You'll find another one."

"It's not the same. When your dog gets killed you can't just get another one and expect that it's the same. What about you. Aren't you sad that Star is gone?"

"It's funny. I feel like we will see each other again. It didn't, I guess it doesn't really feel like an end."

"Do you think she's thinking about me?" said Charlie.

"It's hard to say. Maybe give her a couple of days. Call her when we get back, it will give her plenty of time to think about you."

"What about you? Don't you want to call Star?"

"I'm not sure. Everything is still so fresh in my mind. I don't think it's had a chance to sink in yet."

"You're lucky," said Charlie.

"Jackson said we are going to get our stuff. So we can leave tomorrow."

"Holy shit. Like all of it? That's it? Then we just go home?"

"I guess so. He just said everything will be ready for us tomorrow morning. So I guess we should get some rest tonight, because it sounds like we're leaving."

"I suppose you need to get back to school, don't you?"

"Yeah, school. I've barely thought about it in the last couple of days. A week from now I'm going to be back at my apartment in Madison, getting ready to start school on Monday."

"I don't know if I'm ready to leave," said Charlie. "What do I have to go back to? A shit apartment? A job at a sandwich shop? Video games?"

"It's your life Charlie. You need to do whatever you need to do to be happy."

"Maybe after I get home I'll come back out? Pack all my shit and move back out here. I can see if Jackson will give me a job or something?"

"Yeah, maybe," said Oliver. "I'm going to call my mom."

"Tell her I said hi," said Charlie.

Oliver stepped outside with the sun and the ocean breeze in his face.

∞

"Hello Mom," said Oliver. "Charlie says hi."

"Oh, Charlie. Tell him he's a good boy, will you. Are you home now?"

"No, Mom. We're heading back tomorrow."

"Cutting it a little close, don't you think? You need to get back to school you know."

"I know mom. I'll be fine. We should be back by Tuesday. That should be plenty of time for me to get ready."

"Have you thought about my questions?"

"You mean the 'why am I here?' question?" said Oliver.

"Yes," said his mother.

"I don't know, Mom? How do any of us know why we're here?"

"I am here, Oliver, to take care of you and your brother. I gave birth to you, I raised you and I made sure you had food and clothes and a roof over your head. I gave you all I had. I'm not asking you for anything and I'm not telling you that you owe me. I'm just saying what my job here was. My job is finished, Oliver. I don't have anything left to do here."

"That's fucked up, Mom."

"Oliver, don't use those words."

"Sorry, Mom, but it's messed up to say that your value is gone now that you have finished your production cycle. To say that you don't have value just because I don't need you to feed me is crazy. I still need you, Mom."

"You don't need me, Oliver. It's okay, I'm coming to terms with it. Who really knows why we are here on this earth my son. We are here though, for a period of time. Everything that I have done, I have done. I am proud of what I have done. I am proud of you."

"Every time I talk to you, it sounds like you're giving up. Why don't you fight this?"

"You can't always fight Oliver. Not everything is a battle. You think you are immortal, and that's a product of youth."

"But you're not that old mom. It's not like you're a senior citizen."

"I'm old enough. Always question, Oliver. Always ask the question. Why am I here? The question is more important than the answer. Sometimes the answer is simple. You got here because of the choices you made. What are you going to do now to make a change? Or is this where you are supposed to be and how are you going to be grateful. Always be grateful. The answer can change every day. The meaning of the question can change every day. I don't know the answer for you my son. I know the question. Always ask the question."

"Okay, Mom, okay."

"I have to go now, Oliver. I'm going to Bingo. The cards aren't going to play themselves. I've got to meet Joyce and Alice and get a good spot in the room. If I get there too late I end up on the other side of the hall. I can't see the numbers from there. If Bob Jensen is calling tonight I can barely hear him half the time, even if I'm right next to him. Love you Oliver, got to go."

"I love you too, Mom. I'll see you in a few days."

∞

Oliver stepped from the bright afternoon sun, back into the dimly lit house. Charlie and Jason were sitting on the couch talking and sharing a joint. Jason passed it to Oliver.

"How was your journey last night?" said Jason.

"It was good," said Oliver. "It wasn't what I expected."

"How so?" said Jason.

"I guess I thought I would see things. You know hallucinate, or something. It was more feelings than anything else. I had a lot of interesting thoughts that came from a place that didn't seem like they were coming from my own head. Like there was someone else there showing me, or telling me something."

"Do you remember any of them? Do you remember any of the things that came to you?"

"Sort of, but it might not make a lot of sense now," said Oliver. "I remember being asked if a lion questions its ability to be a lion. Its lion nature. It just takes as it needs. I felt really deeply that it didn't. But it's weird. It wasn't like a question that someone said. It was just kind of there. The other thing that really stood out was that I had a deep desire to be around things that were real and true."

"I thought I was dying for a while," said Charlie. "I really thought I was going to die. I thought I wasn't going to leave this place and I wouldn't be able to come back."

"How do you feel about it now?" said Jason.

"Well, I didn't die," said Charlie. "It was pretty scary though. I guess I feel better about it now. It's still pretty fresh in my mind. I've been thinking about my life a lot, and how precious it really is. We don't really know what's going on here do we? Like, why we're alive? Oliver was talking about it a few days ago, but I didn't really get it until last night."

"Did you close your eyes at all?" said Jason.

"I don't remember?" said Oliver.

"I did," said Charlie. "At one point I laid down and tried to sleep it off. When I closed my eyes all I saw was this big endless kaleidoscope. It was like these colorful fractal patterns that rotated and fell into each other. I decided it was easier to stay awake."

"Interesting," said Jason.

"Is that normal," said Charlie.

"It can be," said Jason. "It's not unusual."

"What does it mean?" said Charlie.

"I don't know. I've seen the kaleidoscope too, but I don't know if it means anything. A scientist might tell you the kaleidoscope is one thing and a mystic might tell you it's another thing. It just is, I guess. Well, I need to be moving along. It was good to meet you guys. Maybe our paths with cross again someday," said Jason, hoisting his pack on one shoulder and shaking their hands with his free arm.

Jason walked out the door and only Oliver and Charlie remained. The house felt suddenly empty, and a little lonely. Charlie grabbed a neatly rolled joint from the table and lit it.

"So what's with the hat? Are you going to bring it with us?" said Charlie.

"I don't know," said Oliver. "I haven't really thought about it. I've been wearing it because Jackson told me too. I kind of like it. Sounds like it's pretty expensive. I don't know if Jackson actually gave it to me or just borrowed it to me."

"It's yours kid," said Jackson emerging from the dark hallway. "Don't wear it while you're driving back. It'll draw too much attention. Are you guys going to be ready by the morning? Pass me that joint."

"We'll be ready," said Oliver.

The rest of the evening seemed to happen in a breeze. Oliver tried to call Jeb with no success. Charlie sat on the couch, watched TV and tried to forget about Megan.

The house was empty except for Oliver and Charlie for the rest of the day. Jackson was out running errands. Chewy and Mia were nowhere to be found.

29

Morning light was sneaking in. Oliver stretched his whole body and felt a slight breeze coming through the window. In the air he could smell fresh pine, hints of the ocean and bacon.

Oliver thought that it would be good to live here. He wished that he didn't have to leave yet, but today was the day. He wondered what it would be like to wake up in this place every morning. To roll out of bed and eat bacon, do a few chores in the garage and go out in the world to have adventures up and down the coast. He wondered what it would be like to wake up next to Mia.

"Morning kid," said Jackson, as Oliver walked into the kitchen.

"Hey," said Oliver. Charlie was already up and eating breakfast at the kitchen counter. Mia and Chewy sat at the little table in the kitchen and drank coffee.

"You're all packed up," said Chewy. "It's under the stow-and-go seating compartments in your van. It's all hidden under the floor."

"You shouldn't have to touch it at all," said Jackson. "At all. Let Jeb take care of it when you get back. Just get back and take the van to him. Don't even look at it."

"Got it," said Oliver.

"I fucking mean it. Leave it alone. You're better to not even think about it. Pretend it's not there if you have to. Completely forget about it," said Jackson.

"Okay," said Oliver.

"You too, Charlie, you fuck," said Jackson.

"What did I do?" said Charlie.

"Nothing," said Jackson. "It just doesn't seem like you're taking this seriously. This is the real fucking ball game boys. This is actually happening. No hippie love bullshit here. If you get busted you're going to be put in hell. How do you want your eggs, Oliver?"

"Easy over. Do you have toast?"

"After you eat breakfast you guys should hit the road," said Jackson. "Drive during the day. Get a hotel at night. No exceptions. It will take a little bit longer, but cops are less suspicious during the day. Do not drive tired."

"Do you have any jobs?" said Charlie. "If I came back, could I work for you again?"

"Maybe," said Jackson. "But not during the winter. If you're serious, call me next spring. I'll keep you in mind."

Oliver ate his breakfast quickly. He could feel his nerves starting to rise, but none of it seemed real. It was almost as if he were in a haze at this point. As if he were going through the motions of being pushed through a tube.

"Before you go, Oliver, I have some makeup for your eye," said Mia. "Come here and let me show you how to put it on."

They walked down the hall and into the bathroom. Oliver looked at his eye in the mirror. The swelling had gone down. It was now just a big black spot with red around the edges about the size of a dime under his eye, with a little black spot on his eye lid that you could see when he closed his eye.

"Does it hurt when I touch it?" said Mia.

"No, not really. The physical pain is pretty much gone. My ego still hurts a little bit," Oliver smiled.

"Just put a little dab on your finger like this, and rub it in," said Mia. "It's very easy."

"Thanks for everything," said Oliver. "You guys have been really good to us. I can't thank you enough."

"Just get home safe," said Mia. "That's how you can thank me. Jackson was really close to your brother. They have been friends for a long time. They are a lot alike, your brother and Jackson. I think he feels protective of you, like an older brother."

"Sometimes I get the feeling that he doesn't like me very much," said Oliver.

"That's just his way. He gave you the hat didn't he?"

"Yeah, why did he give it to me?"

"I don't know. I guess he was done with it. He wore that thing every day for probably a year. Honestly, I'm glad to see it go," said Mia, smiling.

They walked back out to the living room. Chewy and Jackson were sitting on the couch rolling joints. Charlie was sitting on the couch arm.

"Drive safe," said Chewy. "Take it one mile at a time and you will get there just fine."

"Don't be fucking idiots," said Jackson, looking up from his half rolled joint.

"Give me a hug," said Mia, hugging Oliver and kissing him on the cheek. "You too, Charlie."

They stepped from the dimly lit living room into the golden morning. It was about 9 a.m., the sun was bright and there was fog rising off the shore. A couple of sea gulls soared on air currents above the drop off to the beach, just on the other side of the road.

As Oliver walked to the van and sat down in the driver's seat, his heart began to drop into the pit of his stomach. The realization that this was actually happening started to sink in. He turned the van on, put it in reverse and backed out the driveway.

"Are you nervous?" said Charlie.

"Yeah," said Oliver. "It just hit me. This is for real now. When I told Jeb yes, I didn't think this far ahead. I didn't actually picture myself here, now, in the driver's seat doing this."

"We're just driving. No one is looking to pull over a minivan. As long as we follow the rules we'll be fine," said Charlie.

"I know. I just need to try and forget about it. My brother told me to compartmentalize it. Pretend like there is an invisible divider between us and the back of the van. Pretend it's not even there."

29.5

They headed south on Highway 101 past Arcata and Eureka. They were silent for a long time. Through Garberville and out of Humboldt County.

"What a crazy adventure," said Charlie. "I told you we would get laid."

"It was crazy," said Oliver.

"It was amazing. You have to admit it was amazing."

"Yeah, it was pretty amazing."

"Once you stopped bitching," said Charlie.

"It took a little bit for me to wrap my head around it," said Oliver. "I've got a lot going on back home with school and my mom."

"Is your mom going to be okay?" said Charlie.

"No, she's going to die."

"Just like that? Usually the doctor gives someone like a percent chance, like 75% chance of recovery or 30% chance? At least that's the way they make it sound on TV."

"If the doctor gave her something like that she isn't telling me. It sounds like she is just going to let it take her. Like she isn't going to do anything about it."

"That's pretty fucking heavy," said Charlie.

Through Leggett and Willits, and left onto Highway 20. The road gets hilly and curvy and passes by a beautiful lake with vacation homes and boats and tourists, on their last day of vacation before heading home to the city and their 9 to 5 jobs.

"Google Maps says that lake is called Clear Lake. I wonder if there are any fish in there," said Charlie. "I've always wanted to go fishing."

"You've never been fishing? We grew up on the Mississippi river."

"Never did. It's not like my parents were going to take me. Do you ever remember fishing with me?"

"I guess not. My brother and I used to go when I was young. Why didn't you ever come with us?"

"I don't know," said Charlie. "I don't know."

In Williams they headed south on Interstate 5.

"I can't stop thinking about her, Oliver. For real," said Charlie. "I beat off twice in a row in the shower this morning thinking about her."

"That's really persistent," said Oliver. "You're going to have more girlfriends, Charlie."

"It took me 21 years to get this one. If it takes me 21 more years my balls will be all wrinkled up and useless."

"I don't think it works like that, Charlie. Besides, twice your age is 42 and that isn't that old. You can find another one. Now that you have some practice with girls the next one should be easier. Right?"

"I guess so," said Charlie. "Man, she was a freak."

In Sacramento they headed East on Interstate 80.

"This will take us all the way to Iowa," said Oliver.

"That's almost home," said Charlie.

"Yeah, I'm ready to go home," said Oliver. "Don't get me wrong, this has been incredible, but it will feel good to be getting back to normal."

"I don't want to go home. I'm not ready to go home. I don't think I'll ever be ready to go back to that place. It's different for me than it is for you. You have something to do. You have a future. You have options. I don't have anything. I have a shit-hole in the wall apartment and a shit job with no chance of it getting better. You're going to college and when you get out you get to have a career. Slinging sandwiches isn't a career path."

"You need to stop feeling sorry for yourself, Charlie. You had just as much opportunity to go to college as I did. I didn't wake up in this world with a silver spoon in my mouth, in case you didn't notice. I worked hard to get to college. I did what I had to do. You are the only one who can make your life better. Feeling sorry for yourself isn't working."

"It always came easy to you. You always got your homework done. You always got A's in school. I didn't, I was lucky to get a C. It wasn't easy for me like that. I hated it."

"Fuck you, man. I wasn't lucky to get A's. I worked my ass off. It wasn't easy for me. I had to do all of my homework and still had to try and be the man of the house. My brother was gone by the time we got into high school and you know my mom never had a man around. It wasn't easy at all. I did it because that's what I had to do. I had to have a better life than that. I did all my homework assignments, and from what I remember you only did the ones that you wanted to do. Sometimes you just didn't turn shit it. That brings your average way down. It's like you never got it."

"Because it was all bullshit," said Charlie. "I never wanted to go to college anyway. I knew I wasn't good enough for that. College is for smart people. I'm not smart, Oliver."

"That's bullshit. You keep telling yourself that. You actually believe that. That's complete horse shit. It's like this self-doubt demon thing gets in your head every time something challenging gets in front of you, and you need a reason to avoid it. You just tell yourself that you're stupid and that's enough of an excuse to let yourself off the hook. Charlie, you're not stupid. You need to realize this. You need to learn to meet challenges head on and stop making excuses for yourself. No one is going to hand you a ticket for a free ride in this world. I think you have figured that out for yourself by now. If you're not satisfied with the way your life is, then you need to take your life by the balls and move it in the direction you want it to go."

"It sounds so simple when you say it. I just don't know how. I don't know how to do that. I'm not on the same page as you in the story."

"Yes you are, Charlie. You don't have to go to college to be happy with yourself, or to do something meaningful with your life. That's what I'm doing, but you're not me. We're both right here. We're in a car heading in a direction. You just need to keep going in a direction when we get home. Don't just shut yourself into your apartment and wait for something to happen. You need to pick a direction and go with it. Make a goal. When I decided to go to college it was a choice. I did what I had to do to get there and I didn't let myself stray from that path, even when I thought shit was hard I did it anyway. I pushed through. What do you want to do? What do you want to be? It's your choice. We're still young. We can do anything."

"I know... I know this. It's just easier said than done."

"Life isn't always easy, Charlie. It just isn't. Sometimes you have to put in the work. It's not always hard either. Look at the shit we just did. That wasn't that hard. That was pretty awesome, right?"

"I get it. Life's a balance. I get it," said Charlie.

After Sacramento the road headed east into and over the Sierra Mountain Range.

"We'll be in Reno in like an hour," said Oliver. "Do you think we should get a hotel for the night?"

"You're the one who's in a hurry to get back," said Charlie. "I don't have shit to do. We can stop whenever you want."

"It's only like 5 o'clock, but I don't want to be on the road too late," said Oliver. "My nerves are fried as it is."

The sun was far behind them in the distance. Reno seemed like a different world than Northern California. The start of an expansive desert that is yet to be crossed, lights and buildings shouting for attention in the early night sky, rising out of the unforgiving ground.

They found a little average looking hotel just off Interstate 80. Not so small that they were the only ones there, but not so big that it looked expensive. There was a small casino off of the lobby as they went in. Lights flashed and bells chimed as they walked by.

"I bet I can get a hooker here," said Charlie.

"Fuck, Charlie. We got shit to do. We're not here to get hookers. We're not looking for any unwanted trouble."

"I think it's legal here. Don't they have brothels and stuff around here? Dude, we should go to a brothel. Talk about taking our minds off the heavy shit."

"Yeah and how are we going to get there? You plan on driving all over the desert with more than 60 pounds of in weed in our van. Fuck that. Let's just stay here in our hotel and get some rest."

"You're being like the dad I never wanted," said Charlie. "We need to blow off some steam."

"Do whatever you want. I'm going to bed. We need to get up early tomorrow and get on the road."

"I've got a pocket full of money. I'm going for an adventure to get my mind off shit. You coming with me?"

"No," said Oliver. "I'm staying here. I need to get some sleep. We're leaving at 6 a.m. tomorrow."

30

At 6:30 a.m. Charlie walked through the door of the hotel room.

"Did I make it?"

"Dude I told you that we were going to leave at 6 and you stroll in at 6:30? You didn't get any sleep. What the fuck are you doing Charlie? Seriously, what the fuck."

"Well, remember that pocket of money I had? I don't have to worry about that anymore."

"What did you do?"

"Let's just go," said Charlie. "I want to get the fuck outta here. I'll tell you about it in the car."

They drove east into the morning sun. Out of the city and into the desert. The air was chilly, and the dry look to everything around them made them feel very far from home.

"So what did you do last night? What happened to all of your money?" Oliver said, looking over at Charlie who was already passed out in the passenger seat.

The miles ticked by slowly, one-by-one, as Oliver drove headlong into the big ball of sun rising over head. It was almost 1 o'clock in the afternoon and they were crossing the salt flats in Utah when Charlie finally woke up.

"So what the fuck happened to you last night?"

"I don't really want to talk about it," said Charlie. "It sucked. I lost all my money. I got too fucked up. I didn't get a hooker. I didn't even see any boobs."

"How did you lose all your money?"

"So, I went down to the lobby and put $5 into a machine. I won $250 on the second pull. I was stoked. I was like holy shit this is going to be a great night. So I got into a cab and thought about going to a strip club, but decided to go to a casino first. I thought if I won some more money I would have more fun. I was starting to feel really good. So I get to the casino and they have free drinks if you're gambling. I started at the slots and won $100 more dollars in the first 5 minutes. By that time I was thinking that this is the luckiest night of my life. So I get a couple of shots. Then I sat down at the Black Jack table. I've played Black Jack a few times on the computer and it didn't seem that hard. I had like eighteen hundred dollars and I'm pretty sure that's the most money I've ever had in my pocket at one time. There was a hot chick next to me who kept winning. She kept telling me I need to bet big to win big. So I was getting pretty drunk and I put all my cash into chips. I bet a few hands and won a couple, then I decide to put it all in on one hand. I thought if I won I would double my money and it would be awesome. I was on a hot streak. So I pushed all my chips in. I busted. That's when I realized I didn't really know how to play Black Jack."

"So you lost it all? You lost all the money you had? All that money you made from trimming in one hand of Black Jack?"

"Yep."

"So what the fuck did you do all night?"

"I sat there for a little while. I didn't really know what to do? The dealer told me I had to leave the table and the hot chick didn't want to have anything to do with me. I ordered one more drink and tried to sit at the table longer, but they must have known I was out of money. They told me to leave if I wasn't going to play anymore. I didn't have money for a cab. I didn't even know where the hotel was and I was pretty drunk."

"Dude, why didn't you call me?"

"I don't know. I just figured it was my mess and I had to get out of it. So I started walking. I asked directions a couple of times at all night gas stations and liquor stores. I'm just glad I found the hotel."

"That's really messed up," said Oliver.

The sun was finally starting to drift behind them and the afternoon sky was blue and clear. After Salt Lake City the mountains rose from the desert. It was midafternoon and the wind was cool and steady as they passed into Wyoming.

"I'm going to sleep good tonight," said Oliver.

"Are you getting tired," said Charlie.

"I'm tired of driving," said Oliver.

The sun was at their backs as they reached the Continental Divide.

"Check it out," said Charlie. "Remember this from on the way out. We passed through here at night and that van scared the shit out of us. Hey, do you want to stop and take a piss."

"No. I'm good," said Oliver.

"Do you want me to drive a little while," said Charlie.

"No, I've got it. I think if I get out and stretch for a little bit I'll be fine," said Oliver.

31

In the early evening as the sun was cresting over the mountains in the distance behind them Oliver and Charlie stopped for gas in Laramie, Wyoming.

"Come on," said Charlie. "Let me drive for a while. You need a break."

"Maybe we can make it to Cheyenne and get a hotel," said Oliver.

"Well let me drive that far at least," said Charlie.

"I don't know Charlie. This shit is pretty sketchy. I don't know if I could live with myself if, well, you know."

"It's not my first time driving a car, Oliver. I can do this."

After filling up and stretching they got back into the car. Charlie got into the driver's seat and Oliver reclined into the passenger seat and put his feet up on the dash. The sun had set behind them, and there was no more than a hint of orange glow over the horizon in the rear view mirror.

"Just think, Oliver. By this time tomorrow we could be home if we drive long enough," said Charlie to a sleeping Oliver.

32

"Oliver, wake up. Oh fuck, Oliver, you need to wake up now!"

"What? What's going on?"

"Dude, I fucked up."

"What? Where are we?"

"In Nebraska."

"Why the fuck are we in Nebraska?" said Oliver, as he noticed the red and blue lights flashing.

"Dude, I'm so sorry. I just thought I could make it a little farther."

"Calm down Charlie. We have to pull over."

"I'm so sorry Oliver. I'm so sorry."

"You need to pull it together," said Oliver. "We're not busted yet. What did you do?"

"I don't even know? I might have gone over the line just a little bit? I was messing with the radio."

"Just be cool, Charlie. When he comes to the window, just be cool. We haven't been busted yet. It might just be something simple."

Charlie put his blinker on and slowly started pulling the car to the edge of the road. His heart was so far in his stomach it felt like he was sitting on it. Every bone in his body wished it would have played this scenario out differently. There was a metallic taste in his mouth and a ringing in his ears.

"Oliver. If we get busted I'm gonna to take the blame," said Charlie.

"Shut up. We're not going to get busted."

"I will say you didn't know anything about it. I'll say I set up the deal and we were on vacation and you didn't know anything about it."

"That isn't going to happen. Just be cool, Charlie. Please!" Oliver whispered through clenched teeth.

They were fully stopped at the side of the road. The lights flashed in the mirrors and on the dark road to the sides and ahead of them. An officer stepped out of the driver's side of the cop car and another stepped out the passenger side. A semi drove past and the wind gently shook their vehicle.

"Howdy, boys," said the officer at the driver's side window. He was tall and thin and wore a large flat brimmed hat. "Can you open that passenger side window so my partner can have a peek inside?"

Oliver rolled down his window.

"Is there something wrong," said Charlie, with a lump in his throat that felt like a baseball.

"That's exactly what I thought when I saw you swerving back there, son," said the tall officer.

"Have you boys been drinking," said the officer in the passenger window, as he shined his light all over the back of the van. He seemed a little shorter and more round than the officer on the driver's side.

"Where you comin' from?" said the tall officer.

"We're coming from California," said Oliver.

"No one was talking to you," said the round officer.

"I think I'm going to have to ask you boys to step out of the vehicle," said the tall officer.

Flick, flick, flick went the red and the blue.

"What did we do?" said Oliver.

"We'll see about that," said the round officer. "We have our dog with us. He's just going to walk around your car once or twice and tell us. There have been quite a few of you kids coming through these parts since they made pot legal down there in Colorado."

"We have rights," said Charlie. "I know my rights."

"What do you need rights for?" said the tall officer. "If you didn't do anything wrong there shouldn't be a problem."

"I'm going to ask you one more time nicely," said the round officer, with his hand firmly planted on his gun. "Step out of the vehicle and keep your hands where we can see them at all times."

Oliver took a deep breath, and reached for his door handle. He just wanted to crawl into bed. He wished that he was checking into a hotel room right now and laying his head on a pillow. He wished he was home in his bed. He wished this wasn't happening at all. Is this real?

Charlie stepped from the vehicle first and the tall officer led him to the back of the car at gun point. Oliver stepped out of the vehicle and the round officer led him to the front of the car.

"Put your hands on the hood of the van," said the round officer. "I don't want to see them move. Not an inch."

Charlie was standing, legs spread and hands on the hood of the cop car. Another semi drove by and the wind blew Oliver's hair. A van followed closely behind the semi. A van driving down the highway at 75 miles per hour, the people in it are probably comfortable, radio playing, having a nice Conversation.

Another cop car pulled in behind the two vehicles. Time seemed to stop.

"You stay right there boy. Don't you fucking move," the round cop said to Oliver as he walked back to have a conversation with the other officers.

'Maybe this is a dream?' Thought Oliver. 'No. This is the real thing.' His heart pounded in his chest. 'Maybe they won't find anything? Should I run? Fuck, there's nothing for miles. Fuck. Oh fuck.'

The tall officer pulled a dog out of the back his SUV police cruiser. The dog immediately took an interest in the van. It lunged at it. It barked. It jumped up on the side of the vehicle and barked and barked and barked.

"I'm going to have to restrain you son," said the round officer, gun pulled walking back to Oliver, the barrel pointed straight at Oliver's head. "Put your hands behind your back. Slowly."

He cuffed Oliver and brought him around the rear of the vehicle, where Charlie stood already cuffed.

"We are going to search your vehicle," said the tall officer. "Our dog knows you have something in there."

"We have rights," said Oliver.

"What exactly do you have in there?" said the tall officer.

"You can't search our vehicle," said Oliver. "You don't have my permission."

"Who the fuck do you think you are?" said the new officer. "You're driving through our neighborhood now. Our dog says you're in possession of contraband of one type or another. You bet your sweet prison loving ass we are going to find out."

"I'm going to ask politely one more time. You're really close to getting into a resisting arrest situation, even if it's only a joint or a pipe, you're about to spend the night in jail. So, what are we going to find."

"It's mine," shouted Charlie. "It's all fucking mine. All of it."

The new officer opened the sliding door. "It's one of these stow-and-go seating vans. I bet these are nice. Why does it smell like piss in here? Holy shit. We hit the mother load boys," he said pulling a large vacuum sealed bag out of the van and shining it in the headlights. "I bet if the other side is as full as this one, we got a half a million dollar's worth of dope here."

"You fucking kids," said the round officer. "Driving through my country. You make me fucking sick, you little piece of shit faggots. Selling your drugs to my kids. Infecting the whole community with your disease."

"How do you boys feel about prison?" smiled the tall officer.

"I need to get home," said Oliver. "I need to be in school on Monday. I'm going to be a senior in college."

A note from Douglas John Noble

My friends just call me Doug.

Thank you so much for reading Satori Sunset. If you enjoyed it please take a moment to leave a review at your favorite online retailer such as Amazon USA or Amazon UK.

Keep up with my current events and new work.

Facebook: facebook.com/DouglasJohnNoble
Twitter: @dougynoble
Website: douglasjohnnoble.com

While you're at my website join my email list...

My email list will receive notices when I publish and I will pack it with as many bonuses as I can along the way.

Love,
Doug